D0395401

Twig looked around. Just then an amber shaft of afternoon sunlight poked through the clouds and slanted its way across the river, illuminating the jewel-like blossoms and fern fronds on the riverbank. The whole world seemed bathed in gold. The sun slanted down some more, and Twig blinked.

Something caught his eye. Twig sat up, looking more closely. It glinted in the mud and sand where water had eroded the riverbank.

It was perfect. It seemed to glow, smooth and flawless. He knew that no one in the Hill, no one, had ever seen the likes of it.

ALSO BY HENRY COLE

MIDDLE GRADE

Brambleheart #2: Bayberry Island
A Nest for Celeste: A Story About Art,
Inspiration, and the Meaning of Home

PICTURE BOOKS

I Took a Walk
Jack's Garden
On Meadowview Street
On the Way to the Beach
Trudy

HENRY COLE

Brambleheart

A Story About Finding Treasure and the Unexpected Magic of Friendship

KATHERINE TEGEN BOOKS
An Imprint of HarperCollins Publishers

Katherine Tegen Books is an imprint
of HarperCollins Publishers.

Brambleheart
Copyright © 2016 by HarperCollins Publishers
All rights reserved. Printed in the United States of America.
No part of this book may be used or reproduced in any manner
whatsoever without written permission except in the case of brief
quotations embodied in critical articles and reviews.
For information address HarperCollins Children's Books,
a division of HarperCollins Publishers,
195 Broadway, New York, NY 10007.
www.harpercollinschildrens.com

Library of Congress Cataloging-in-Publication Data
Cole, Henry, date.
    Brambleheart / Henry Cole. — First edition.
        pages   cm
    Summary: A young apprentice chipmunk in a guild of crafts
animals strikes up an unlikely relationship with a dragon who
teaches him the meaning of true friendship.
    ISBN 978-0-06-224544-1
    [1. Chipmunks—Fiction. 2. Dragons—Fiction. 3. Forest
animals—Fiction. 4. Friendship—Fiction. 5. Fantasy.] I. Title.
PZ7.C67345Br   2016   2014048578
[Fic]—dc23   CIP
                                                       AC

Typography by Carla Weise
19 20 21   CG/LSCH   10 9 8 7 6
❖

First paperback edition, 2017

For Biscuit and Mullet

Contents

chapter 1

Twig

Twig made his way to class, in the rain. It was a cold, late-spring rain, which soaked into his fur with a chill. A gray sky of leaden clouds hung over the Hill like a drab, wet quilt.

Plink! Splot! The raindrops hit the metal and plastic junk that made up the giant Hill. It surrounded Twig as he scooted around and through the familiar assortment of human refuse.

He paused outside the Burrow of Weaving. A notice

1

had been posted outside, a reminder of the upcoming Naming Ceremony, as if anyone needed to be reminded.

The Naming Ceremony was the most important day at the Hill. At the end of their Naming Year, every graduating student would be given their final names. The names signified mastery of a subject and would determine what job and status the graduates would have in Hill society. Soon, Twig's friends would be named Weavers and Metal Crafters and Carvers. Twig hoped he would be named something.

Twig slipped into the classroom. His chipmunk nose twitched gratefully as he saw his friend Lily gesture to him, pointing to the seat beside her. He scrambled onto the wooden bench.

"Professor Fern is going to call for demonstrations this morning," Lily whispered. "I'm all set. If she calls on me, I'm demonstrating either the Cloud Knot or the Burr Knot. I can't decide."

Twig smiled. Either knot was extremely difficult, but he knew that if anyone could tie them, Lily could.

"What about you, Twig?"

"I thought I'd try the Sparrow Knot."

"That's an easy one!"

"For you, maybe."

Lily's nose wiggled. "Did you study your *Knot Manual* last night?" she asked.

Twig turned pink at the tips of his furry ears.

"Uh-huh . . . just as I thought," Lily sighed. "Looking at your picture books instead of studying. Really, Twig. You need to put your whiskers in the Manuals."

Just then Professor Fern slapped her tail. She was

large, even for a beaver. Her thick brown fur was always at least a little damp and smelled of marsh weeds and pond water. She kept a stash of fresh willow twigs next to her desk and was constantly peeling and nibbling the bark off them.

She smiled patiently as the students settled in. "All right," she called out. "Everyone quiet, please. We've got a few demonstrations this morning, and then a small pop quiz after."

Everyone groaned.

Phoebe piped up. "You didn't tell us there was going to be a quiz!" she squeaked, and nervously fidgeted with her pink tail.

Professor Fern smiled, chewing a willow stem. "If I announced it, it wouldn't be a pop quiz, now, would it? Okay, let's see. Lily? How about you for our first demonstration? Do you have a knot you'd like to show us?"

Lily stood, like most rabbits, erect and alert, with sharp eyes and soft, tawny ears. Her fur was a mottled mix of cinnamon brown and pearl gray, except for her paws and tail, which were as white as moonlight on a snowbank.

Lily was almost certainly destined to be named Master Weaver. Ever since she was young, she'd practiced at working strands of grass or string or nylon cord into amazingly strong and intricate ropes. She  could weave any fiber into rope as strong as an ironwood branch, or as delicate as a moth's antenna.

As expected, Lily's demonstration went smoothly. She tied the Cloud Knot with no mistakes. Her coral-colored nose wiggled as the nimble paws went this way and that.

Professor Fern looked pleased, beaming at the

perfectly formed knot. She slapped her tail on the floor. "Excellent, Lily," she said. "I would be proud to have executed such a difficult knot as well as this. You are most certainly to be named Master Weaver at the upcoming Ceremony."

"Thank you, Professor Fern," Lily replied, blushing.

Twig sighed. His chances at Master Anything looked fairly bleak. He was barely good enough to keep up. And this third and final year of training was the toughest yet, with projects and assignments popping up like mushrooms after a spring rain.

He tried to hide in the back of the room behind Hyacinth, hoping to be overlooked as the next presenter.

Professor Fern called on Ivy, a young wood rat, who created a satisfactory example of an Owl Knot. Though not very difficult, it was an unusual knot.

"Good, Ivy. Peeper?"

There was an awkward moment when Peeper stumbled for a moment while tying a Snail Knot, but he recovered to finish nicely.

Basil the weasel did a passable job tying a Double Branch Knot but got distracted when Twig sneezed. "That was easy," he announced when he completed the knot, but as he sat down, he glared at Twig. "Idiot!" he whispered.

"Okay," Professor Fern said. "Next we'll have . . . uh . . . how about you, Twig?"

Twig gulped.

He picked up two ropes and began his Sparrow Knot, but quickly became all left toes, flustered and confused. The ropes became a jumbled tangle.

"No, wait . . . ," Twig mumbled, trying to loosen the knot and start over. "Let's see, right over left, around . . . through . . . and back? No . . . uh . . ."

Professor Fern sighed, interrupted him. "Twig, perhaps you should have a seat." Looking disappointed, she took the confusing mass of rope and tossed it in the bin marked *To Untangle*. "If I were you, Twig, I would spend tonight memorizing." She gestured at a copy of *20 Basic Knots* lying on her desk. "And I mean memorizing *well*. You need to be skilled at those before you can advance in here."

"Yes, Professor Fern," said Twig.

"Now, everyone, pencils out for the pop quiz."

Twig handled the quiz without too much problem; it consisted of true-or-false questions about threads and yarns. But afterward the professor pulled Twig to one side.

"Twig, dear, really . . . you need to pay more attention in class!" she said, leaning over the chipmunk. Twig could smell her duckweed scent. "I'm afraid your work isn't up to the quality we're striving for here on the Hill." She chewed and munched some more, looking serious. "You want to be *powerful*, don't you? That's what being a Master means. It means being able to *build* things . . . so you can *trade* things . . . and *own* things."

Twig looked dejectedly at the floor.

"The Sparrow Knot demonstration today," Professor Fern continued. "A perfect opportunity for you to shine! But . . . well, I don't think your heart was in it. I know that you want to be a part of the Naming Ceremony, but at this point you wouldn't even be considered. I can hardly imagine what your mother would say if after three years of training you remain . . . nameless!"

Twig gulped hard. Not receiving a last name would mean never becoming a respected member of the Hill. "No name . . . ?" he asked incredulously.

Professor Fern stopped her chewing and looked thoughtfully at Twig. "I'm afraid your father would be very disappointed in you, Twig. He was so respected on the Hill, such a brilliant Metal Crafter, and you . . . well . . ."

Twig's tail sagged.

Professor Fern looked apologetic but said firmly, "If your work doesn't improve, and I'm certainly hoping it will, I will have to suggest to the Hill Council that you be . . . trained as an Errand Runner."

Twig looked up, wide-eyed. Errand Runner! It was the lowest of all positions on the Hill. Errand Runners spent their lives toiling over trivial, tedious chores: delivering scrap metal, stoking glass furnaces, untangling knots.

"Professor Fern," Twig yelped. "I'll learn those knots tonight, honest! But please don't give my name to the Council as Errand Runner."

"I'm sorry, Twig," she answered, putting her damp paw on his shoulder. "That's the recommendation I would have to make."

Twig's tail sagged even lower. "Yes, ma'am," he said despondently. He left the Weaving classroom with ears drooped, tail dragging.

chapter 2
Incident in Metal Craft

Errand Runner. It meant fetching, carrying, empty-ing trash, doing all the little thankless jobs that never end. He could picture Basil and the others order-ing him around, giving him odd and silly tasks to do, belittling and humiliating him.

He wandered through the forest of mayapples that surrounded the Hill, passing the Burrow of Manual Storage. The burrow held every Instruction Manual that had been collected by Hill inhabitants since ancient

13

times, Manuals written by the Two Legs. There were stacks and stacks of materials with labels like *Ace Vacuum Cleaner Operation and Maintenance* and *Know Your Lawn Mower.*

The burrow was held sacred and always kept orderly and clean, but nothing there interested Twig. He preferred his own collection of picture books, and he wished he were home, immersed in the stories.

His daydreaming was broken by Lily's soft voice coming from behind him. "Twig! You look lost. Aren't you going to Metal Craft?" she asked.

"Huh? Oh . . . yeah," groaned Twig. "Metal Craft. Another reason to get yelled at. Another reason to become an Errand Runner."

Lily looked at him sympathetically. "Come on," she chirped, and gestured with her soft ears at the Burrow of Metal Craft. "This afternoon might be better. I'll be your partner. It'll be fine. You'll get a name, I'm sure of it."

They entered the burrow and donned the thick

leather aprons.

Here Professor Burdock
was writing the day's classwork on
the slate board. He had a slender weasel
body and a pinched face with pointy teeth and
ears. He was an important member of the Hill, and next
in line as head of the Hill Council.

He grinned as he saw his nephew Basil enter the burrow. "Ah! The next Master Metal Crafter!" he said loudly. Basil smugly sat at his seat in the front.

An Errand Runner, a graying and thin-bodied vole, tottered into the room through the service tunnel, carrying lead scraps and other materials for the professor.

He padded back and forth between the stockroom and the classroom with a blank expression. Burdock's whiskers twitched with disdain, but the sight of the vole filled Twig with gloom.

The class sat and listened while Professor Burdock gave instructions. "Watch closely as the lead melts in your crucibles," he said sternly. "It will glisten slightly, and wiggle and jiggle a bit as it melts. Be extremely cautious as you pour the liquid lead into the casting form. Melted lead is heavy . . . and very hot."

Twig had no problem melting the lead; with its relatively low melting point, heating it was easy. But next came pouring the molten metal into a form. Professor Burdock handed Twig and Lily a small, decoratively shaped ceramic dish. After the lead had cooled back into a solid, they would have a tiny lead bird.

Lily carefully heated the lead chunk until it crumpled and was rendered into a dull, silvery puddle.

Iris and Basil were at the adjoining workplace. Basil watched as Twig took the tongs and gingerly picked up the crucible of melted metal. "Hey, Deer Toes," he said. "Careful you don't spill any!"

"Steady as she goes," Lily said, ignoring Basil's taunts. "Steady . . . steady . . . you want me to do it?"

"I can do it!" Twig said. "You're making me nervous!"

Lily turned to the side and set about putting out the flame. Twig's paws were shaking as he carried the heavy, hot, smoking metal over to the mold. Just then Basil stuck his foot in front of Twig. Twig stumbled slightly, and hot metal flew through the air, landing on the wooden table, popping and sizzling in all directions. One tiny glob landed on Iris's paw.

"AHH!" the young squirrel squealed with pain as the molten metal burned through her fur. Professor Burdock raced over with some cool water, while the others in the class stared at poor Iris.

"Iris! I'm so sorry!" squeaked Twig. "Let me help you!" He reached for a wet cloth.

"I think you've done quite enough," Professor

Burdock said sharply, baring his pointy teeth at Twig and grabbing the cloth. "The rest of the class, keep working. Lily, you can continue with the exercise, solo. Twig, you are to leave immediately."

"I'm sorry, Professor Burdock. I tripped and—"

"There is no room in my classroom for incompetence."

"But it wasn't my fault! I tripped over Ba—"

"We will discuss this later. Get your things together and go. Now."

Twig glanced at Lily, who looked at him with sympathy. "One step closer to Errand Runner," he sighed to himself.

chapter 3

A Bowl of Soup

O utside, the rain had stopped, but everything was still gray. Twig's head was as clouded as the sky.

The Hill, a human-made mountain of plastic and glass and rust and rubber, loomed all around him, making him feel even smaller. It wound through the Woods, surrounded by trees, shrouded by brambles and vines.

This was his home. This was where he and his family and the rest of the Hill inhabitants lived, existing by scavenging and reconfiguring what the humans, or Two

Legs, had discarded. But he felt like a stranger among the ridges and valleys of the Hill.

Twig spotted an old groundhog, some distance away, who wrestled with a rusted pot and then pulled it from the pile.

A Master Metal Crafter, Twig thought, sighing gloomily, as he watched the grinning groundhog haul the pot away. "Everyone who's been Named is a *some-body*. Has a chance at greatness. And I'm going to be a great . . . nothing."

He saw a pair of deer grazing on tender under-brush. They looked up at him and blinked blankly. Twig envied their simple life: eating, sleeping . . . no pressure to read Manuals or build or be trained or be Named or even be a part of the Hill. Just walk around on their inefficient hooves and chew the vegetation.

His own life seemed so complicated.

Heading home, he took the long way. There was no need to get there quickly; he could already see the disappointed look on his mother's face after he told

her of the day's
events.

Then, like it
sometimes hap-
pens in spring,
the cool, dreary clouds
began to burn away, and
the sun emerged, golden and
huge and warm. It pulled every
sweet, moist smell from the earth
into the air. Birds were singing deep
in the trees in all directions, and bees darted past,
searching for honeysuckle, locust, and wild cherry
blossoms.

Twig had never seen so many different shades of
green, vivid and electric, and felt that he could almost
hear the new leaves popping out of tree buds. It was
as though the day was right out of one of his picture
books . . . beautiful and magical. He half expected a
mythical creature to come swooping out of the trees.

His mood brightened a bit. He couldn't help but wonder how perfect the spring day would be if he hadn't just been humiliated at school.

Eventually the path ended at his home, a pile of broken and cracked crockery, tossed in a heap and cascading down a slope, but transformed into a cozy maze of rooms. It was at a far end of the Hill, away from most of the Hill activity, surrounded by birdsong and wildflowers.

He turned the brass knob of the front door. Inside, something warm and wonderful was being created on the stove; the air was infused with delicious smells. He listened for sounds of Olive, his mother, and cocked his ears toward the kitchen.

The kitchen was an inviting spot, with everything in its place. Utensils hung in logical arrangements next to the oven, pots hung according to size from a beam in the ceiling. There was a small wooden table, usually draped in a piece of colorful cloth, two stools, and one carved chair. The chair had belonged to Twig's father, Mullein. Olive kept it neatly polished.

Adjacent to the kitchen was Olive's workroom: chisels and hammers and other supplies decorated the walls and shelves. She was a Master Stone Carver.

To the other side of the kitchen was Olive's sleeping room. One of its walls backed up to the oven wall, so the room was toasty and snug in winter. Olive had made the acorn-patterned quilt that decorated the bed.

Just as Twig's mother's room was the definition of neatness, Twig's room was that of chaos. It was Mullein's old workroom, and Mullein had been a scavenger: piles of parts littered the floor, covered shelves, and were strewn across bed and chair. Coils of wire hung like strange birds' nests from ceiling hooks. There were gears, knobs, switches, electric motors, scraps of copper, nails and screws, nuts and bolts, hooks and clamps, old jar lids, broken parts of clarinets and accordions, bits of candles, pencil stubs, and the remains of telephones, electric mixers, doorbells, and clocks.

And there was Twig's own collection: a stack of books filled with stories and pictures of mythological sea monsters and dragons. Twig would spend countless hours scouring the Hill until he found one, sometimes worn and torn, or wet and mildewed. To the others who lived on the Hill, and valued only the Manuals, the picture books were just a silly waste of time. But to Twig they were captivating and enchanting. He devoured them. He couldn't get enough.

In the middle of the mayhem was Twig's bed, a plastic tub padded with milkweed down. Sometimes

he slept with an illustrated book of fanciful beasts spread open on top. His favorite picture book was almost always propped against his bed, ready for the umpteenth reading.

Twig tiptoed past Olive's studio. Olive was deep in concentration as she chipped away at a chunk of white marble. A pot of soup bubbled on the kitchen stove; Twig could smell the wild onions, mushrooms, and herbs permeating the air in an aromatic blend. Olive looked up.

"You're home," she chirped. "Hungry? Soup's about ready."

"Okay," Twig replied.

"Go wash up."

He stepped into a tiny alcove that served as a wash-room. Twig carefully washed his paws, taking his time. He could see that his mother was having a great afternoon, immersed in her carving. Describing his grim day would dampen her mood, so he decided to tell her about the classroom disaster another time. He dried his paws on a scrap of bright-red cloth, sighed, and went back to the kitchen.

Olive looked at the wall clock. "Aren't you home a little early?" she asked, with one eyebrow cocked.

"Oh," Twig hedged, scratching his furry ear absently. "There was some sort of accident in Metal Craft. I got out early."

"Accident? Anything serious?"

"Um . . . not really. Want me to set the table?"

"That would be wonderful. Thank you, Twig." Olive began ladling out a bowl of the savory, steaming soup. "This should be pretty good. I used morels I picked this morning . . . plump from the rain."

Twig sipped the delicious soup. It was heavenly. For a moment he was lost in the fragrant broth and tender chunks of morel.

Then his eyes rested on the brown feather that Olive had placed high on a shelf. Twig knew it was from a hawk, the hawk that had taken his father many months before. The day's events sat again on his heart, and the thought of being passed over in the Naming Ceremony. He so wanted to make the spirit of his father proud, but that seemed less and less likely.

His stomach twisted, and he lost all his appetite.

chapter 4

Errand Runner?

Olive poked her whiskers around his bedroom curtain. "Time to get up, Twig!" she said cheerfully. "Peppermint tea and dogwood berry pancakes."

Twig stretched a morning stretch, his tail and paws curling. For a moment he lay staring at the ceiling. Another day of dealing with school; at least Lily would be in both of the day's classes.

He splashed cold water on his face at the basin and combed the white whiskers. He studied himself in the mirror. His eyes held no sparkle. Today he would have to deal with Basil, who was very good in Metal Craft; there would be Basil's showing off, Basil's belittling comments.

Instead of attacking the berry pancakes with his usual gusto, Twig picked at his breakfast. Olive eyed him worriedly.

"Anything on your mind?" she asked, wiping a dish dry.

He poked at the plump red dogwood berries that popped from his pancake. "School . . . Basil . . . everything," he said simply.

"Well, your job is to do your best in class. Concentrate on what you're learning. And ignore Basil. He's not worth worrying over."

Twig ate one more bite of pancake and then slung his leather tool bag across his striped back. "Easier said than done, Mom," he sighed, and he headed off to Welding.

Down the path his ears perked up when he discovered Beau, sitting on a tin can, paws on his cane. Beau had

been
a teacher,
in fact had taught
both Olive and Mullein when
they were youngsters. Now, as the
eldest member of the Hill, he was the
well-respected head of the Council. He had
been like a grandfather to Twig after the loss of Mullein.

Beau's eyes were closed as he sniffed the morning air, smiling absently, enjoying the beginnings of a spring day. Twig was reluctant to interrupt Beau's peaceful moment but wanted to say hello to the old raccoon.

"Good morning, Beau," he said quietly, rolling up another tin can.

"Ah! Twig, my boy," he said warmly. "Heading off to school? Too sweet a morning to be shut up in a classroom, eh?" He scratched behind his ragged ear.

"I'll say," Twig replied.

"What do you have? Electricity? Wood Carving?"

"Worse. Welding."

The raccoon gave a little barking laugh. "I know how you love that one."

Twig poked a stick into the soft ground. "Were you good in school, Beau?"

The raccoon looked up into the trees thoughtfully. His eyes were dark and watery. "See that bird, Twig? Way up there? That was me. Always exploring, poking around . . . paying no mind to anyone."

Twig squinted up into the trees. "Did you get into trouble for that?"

"Well," Beau replied. "The truth is, I don't remember. But I was happy poking around and exploring. Learned a lot. The thing to do is be happy with what you are, whether it's a Metal Crafter or a Welder . . . or an Errand Runner."

Twig sat thinking.

Beau tapped his cane on the ground. "Found a new storybook for you, Twig," he said. "Lots of pictures of magical creatures. Yours anytime."

Twig smiled, feeling better. "Thanks, Beau. I should get going."

"Make it a good day," the raccoon barked as Twig

trotted down the path, his tail flicking. "And tell that Lily I said hello," he added, grinning.

WELDING STARTED OUT WELL ENOUGH. EVERYONE copied down the usual take-home assignment from the slate board before beginning the laboratory experiment. Professor Dunlin stood in front of the class, holding a wooden pointer. Dunlin was a barrel-chested badger with huge, wiry eyebrows. He was a Master Welder for the Hill. His leather apron was blackened and speckled from a history of burns and sparks.

"Does everyone have a partner for our lab exercise?" he asked.

Twig smiled and exchanged a quick glance with Lily, who sat next to him expertly sketching the diagram from the Bellows Instruction Manual into her notebook.

"Ah . . . the bellows," Professor Dunlin said. "You must keep the flow of air steady and at just the right volume. Air in here as the handle is pulled up; air out here through this funnel when the handle is pushed

down. Air in, air out . . . like breathing . . . till the coal burns white hot."

Twig reached over and drew flames engulfing Lily's bellows drawing. Lily giggled.

"Twig . . . Lily . . . a question?" Professor Dunlin asked sharply, his bushy eyebrows raised in an arch.

"No, sir," Twig replied weakly. He felt his ears redden.

"To continue. Once your fire is hot enough, you have the power to become a Master Welder! Now, let's practice with the bellows, taking turns with your partner. Watch the coals; don't let them get too close to the bellows."

Small piles of embers glowed and faded, glowed and faded, as Dunlin walked slowly among the novices, watching them practice.

"Too fast, Sorrel . . . slow and steady as she goes. More elbow grease, Iris! You're not putting enough weight into it!"

Twig watched as Lily took her turn at the bellows

first, working diligently and patiently adding to her coal until she had a white-hot furnace going.

"Excellent!" Dunlin crowed. "Lily, you are quite the pro already. You might even be a contender at the Naming Ceremony."

Lily continued her slow pumping of the bellows. "Thank you, Professor," she said, blushing. "It's not too difficult, once you get the rhythm of it going."

"Quite right," said Dunlin. He licked his paws and stroked his gray whiskers.

But then it was Twig's turn.

Lily was a hard act to follow, and Twig was nervous even before he began. A little overanxious, he pushed the bellows so hard that some hot coals blew across the workspace, almost hitting Lily.

"Twig!" she squeaked. "You want to burn the place down? Start off slowly!" She choked at the gust of ash.

Twig could feel the hot coals burn his cheeks. "Slow and steady, slow and steady," he murmured to himself. Try as he did, his small cluster of coals never progressed. Finally, after accidentally placing the tip of the air intake too close to the coals, and pulling up on the bellows, Twig sucked in some of the hot embers. Soon a stinky yellow-brown smoke began pouring out as the leather began to smolder, then burn. A pungent haze quickly filled the room.

"Open the doors! The windows!" Professor Dunlin screeched.

Coughing and gasping, the students raced outside, with Twig choking from the smoke, and from embarrassment.

Thick smoke billowed out of the classroom window. Several of the teachers could be heard inside, smothering the fire with buckets of sand. Professor Dunlin pedaled a ventilation fan inside, and soon more puffs of the smoke poured out. Twig felt his cheeks burn, sensing the stares of his classmates.

"You're a complete idiot," muttered one of the students as they huddled together. "You . . . again! Don't
you ever do anything right?"

Twig glanced over to see with no surprise that it
was Basil, glaring at him with sooty black eyes, hackles
raised. Everyone heard Basil's remark, and there were
nods and murmurs of agreement. Twig felt himself redden even more. Lily gave him an encouraging, although
helpless, smile.

A small crowd of Hill inhabitants had
gathcred, gawking with curiosity; Twig
was relieved to see his mother
was not among them.
He tried hiding

among the crowd of students and prepared himself for what he knew was coming.

"Twig!" It was Professor Dunlin's voice.

"Yes, sir?" Twig squeaked.

"The whole morning is wasted because of your negligence," Dunlin said. "You need to pay more attention to what you're doing!"

"Yes, sir. I'm very sorry, sir."

Suddenly another voice growled from the edge of the crowd.

"Well, well! What a surprise . . . another failed project from Twig!" The class turned to see Professor Burdock.

His breath smelled of wild garlic and crawfish as he leaned in to Twig. "Tell me," he said. "Would you like your Failure now, or at the end of the semester?"

The others in the class giggled. Burdock glanced casually over the group with a smug grin.

Twig swallowed, churning with embarrassment on the inside.

"Please, Burdock, next time I will—"

"I doubt very much there will be a next time. It is my intention to suggest to the Hill Council that you be demoted to Errand Runner, permanently."

Twig's head was swimming. For the second time in as many days, the threat of Errand Runner had been thrown at him. He looked at Professor Dunlin hopefully, but the old badger's gray eyes were solemn. "You may go now, Twig," he said quietly.

Burdock stood next to the badger. "As for the rest of the class," the weasel snapped, "let this be a lesson to you all: becoming a Master Craftsman allows for no failures or accidents." He glanced at his nephew Basil and grinned. "The cream always rises to the top."

chapter 5

Running Away

Twig wandered aimlessly, pausing near the Hill gates. Nearby was an ancient statue of Arbutus Yardbuilder, the founder of the Hill and its most famous figure. The statue depicted him holding sheets of paper, with one hand pointing, as if giving directions.

Twig stared at the statue. "Tell me where I should go, what I should be," he murmured.

Reluctantly, he started for home.

Tomorrow I will probably be yelled at by Professor Burdock, he thought to himself. *And then forced out of the Guild Master Classes. And then I'll become an Errand Runner . . . an outcast.*

He looked up at the tall trees and thick understory that surrounded him. It was a bit scary, but also mysterious and inviting. He ventured farther into the Woods.

The drooping leaves hung over Twig like a cloak. He crept past the outskirts of the Hill and then past Beau's cottage. Beau had created a cozy spot far from the bustle of life on the Hill, at the base of a beech tree.

A thicket of jack-in-the-pulpit and honeysuckle surrounded the front door, which had been salvaged from an old clock. It was decorated with a bright painting of a cuckoo on a glass panel, and a brass knob. For a moment the warmth of Beau's kitchen beckoned him. He remembered the many evenings the two of them had sat eating muffins and berries by the steamy kitchen window.

He was tempted to tap on Beau's door. No doubt Beau would have welcomed him in, pulling out the carved wooden stool, unwrapping a wild cherry biscuit, and putting the kettle on to boil. But Twig was in no mood for conversation.

He wandered on. Eventually all the familiar trees, rock formations, slopes and valleys, fern patches, rotting logs, trickling streams, and shelf fungi disappeared behind him. His heart raced a bit; he didn't know where he was going, but it felt good to be alone. He quietly scrambled through the thickets and brambles of the Hill, heading east. No one saw him.

He came to a bridge, woven from old leather bootlaces and knotted lengths of baler twine. It had been strung years ago by the Hill's Master Weavers and suspended high above a ravine. He started across.

Midway, Twig peered over the swinging rope rails and studied the tangle of debris far below. Tall weeds and tree saplings had sprouted among the rusted carcass of an old machine, and the persistent push of growth had raised up part of it, as though it was throwing up a tree. Scavengers from the Yard had been here; Twig could see parts had been long ago unscrewed or removed.

To one side lay the mostly

decayed remains of what Twig figured to be a deer, with bone, hooves, and bits of brown fur hiding beneath a blanket of mayapples. Twig shivered and scrambled to the far side of the bridge.

Where the bridge ended, a tunnel began. Twig cautiously entered, the dark, hollow space swallowing him.

Inside the tunnel, he tiptoed around pools of collected rainwater, as he followed one curving space to another, his eyes adjusting to the dim light. It was a good way to remain hidden from hawks and owls when traversing over this part of the Hill.

Twig had been in the tunnel while on a day trip

with his father, and it had marked the farthest he had ever been from home . . . until now. He remembered the dark curves and turning walls of the tunnels. His father had squeezed Twig's paw reassuringly as they explored the tunnel together. "We'd better head back," his father had said when they had reached the end. "Can't let the Dark Creatures catch us." And they had turned home. Twig was suddenly overcome with the wish to have his father next to him again.

Emerging from the tunnel, he breathed in the sweet smell of the forest. The edge of his universe spread before him. Now each step forward was one step into new territory, and one step farther from home.

He passed something huge and ancient, the top of it tilted and its thick carved legs splayed and half-buried in the weeds and soil. Years of rain and snow had battered the once-lustrous mahogany to a matted gray. Mosses and lichens had found the perfect home. Black-and-white pieces, swollen and warped and peeling, ran up one side of the top in a pattern. A festoon of pokeweed jutted out from beneath a sagging lid.

Twig stepped lightly and cautiously onto one of the white pieces. It sank beneath him. Somewhere in the bowels of the sodden, three-legged behemoth something moved, and struck a rusting wire. A sadly muffled note filtered through the decaying wood and hung softly in the evening air.

He stepped again, onto a black piece, and a white one, then another. No sound emerged. The next step made a sound that was loud and strong, startling Twig, and he scampered off into the tall weeds.

He climbed over split and rotting boards, old broken bottles and rusty wires, finally passing through a suspension bridge converted from an old vacuum cleaner hose. There, he came to a small sign, facing the other direction.

Entering the Hill, it read. *All visitors report to Authorities.*

So, Twig thought. *I have reached the edge of the Hill.*

He knew he was in new territory when the very smell of the air was unfamiliar. There was a strange new scent. He didn't recognize it. It was carried on the breeze that caressed his face, luring him on. He had never ventured this far from home. In fact, no one he knew had been this far, not even his father.

The thought sent a shiver through him. Being in this unknown, unfamiliar spot seemed better than the prospect of becoming an Errand Runner.

It felt fine to run away.

chapter 6

Something Marvelous

He scampered up a fallen log and looked ahead. He could sense an expanse of light, just a tree's-length away, where the forest seemed to end.

As he maneuvered around piles of broken fence boards and old plastic bottles and climbed over the massive roots of an ancient sycamore, he poked his head through a clump of maidenhair fern . . . and nearly stumbled off a cliff.

Twig gasped in surprise: the whole hillside dropped off in front of him, a dizzying vertical drop. He'd never been so high; he'd only seen the world from the forest floor.

He looked down, down, down. . . . An enormous expanse of water lay before him, a river of gray and green and blue and brown that rippled and gurgled and sang. He had heard of this before, a river, and had seen illustrations of rivers in his collection of books, but could never have imagined the beauty, or the enormity, of a river.

Large birds were calling to one another in a cascade of white, wings constantly tilting and balancing. They seemed to float on a suspended, invisible river themselves, and Twig stared at them in wonder.

And the breeze! It flowed all around Twig like a magical silk cloth. There was sweetness to it, and a rich earthiness, and honeysuckle, and roses, and a hundred other smells Twig couldn't name. He stood there for some time, overwhelmed.

He stepped out of the tangle of pokeweed and wild roses to get a better view of the river vista. Suddenly the earth gave way beneath his feet. The overhanging embankment collapsed, eroded away for years by the flowing river.

"Help!" Twig yelled uselessly. He clawed at anything within reach as he became part of a landslide of soil and rock and vegetation that swept him down the slope toward the river.

With a splash Twig was pitched into the river.

A snarl of weed stalks, roots, and dirt entangled him, dragging him under. He opened his mouth to squeak, but it only let in a large mouthful of water and soil, and he choked and spat, clawing at the flotsam of vines, stalks, and muddy leaves. The river current was strong, pulling him downriver, quickly turning him over and over like a pinecone tossed down a hillside.

The current pushed him up, and his head emerged briefly at the surface. He gasped wildly for a breath. "Help!" he squeaked, his mouth again filling with water, his body pushed and pummeled and pulled again by the current.

With a sudden *thump*, Twig was washed into something large and heavy in the water. It was an old, sodden tree stump, floating heavily, mostly submerged, covered with slippery algae. Twig climbed on top of it, spitting up water and dirt.

The waterlogged tree stump floated steadily down the river. After a while, the river widened, and the trees could no longer touch their brothers and sisters on the opposite side. Twig pulled a floating weed stalk out of the water and tried to pole the makeshift craft, and was only slightly successful at maneuvering it toward the bank.

He looked ahead, downriver. A supple-looking sapling had been partially uprooted by the current and was bending, arched and stretched, over the river, dangling in Twig's path.

In a moment the sodden log swept by the young tree, whose leaves were tantalizingly close. Twig quickly gathered his strength, tensed his muscles, and leaped.

His weight pulled at the sapling, and for a second Twig thought he might be dunked again in the water. But he scrambled up the branch and down the trunk, and made it to the muddy bank.

Twig felt the warm mud beneath his body and breathed in deeply.

He looked around. Just then an amber shaft of afternoon sunlight poked through the clouds and slanted its way across the river, illuminating the jewel-like

blossoms and fern fronds on the riverbank. The whole
world seemed bathed in gold. The sun slanted down
some more, and Twig blinked.

Something caught his eye. Twig sat up, looking
more closely. It glinted in the mud and sand
where water had eroded the riverbank.

About twice his size, it looked to
be a gold ball, slightly dimpled on
one end. It was luminous, like it
was lit from within. Twig couldn't
tell whether its glow was from the
setting sun hitting it or from the
sphere itself.

But as Twig marveled at it, he
noticed it was slipping slowly, then start-
ing to roll, down the steep embankment, down toward
the dark water, carried by a landslide of soil. On impulse,
he raced to it, pushing upward with his shoulder, trying to
keep it from sliding. His paws slipped, and for a moment
it looked as though he would end up in the river again.

Pushing with all his weight and muscle, Twig moved the golden orb inch by inch up the embankment, until it rolled safely into the grass. He sighed, brushing the bits of dirt and leaves from behind his ears and between his toes. He wiped the golden ball, rubbing it with his furry arms, shining it to a gloss, and then stood back, staring at it.

It was perfect. It seemed to glow, smooth and flawless. He knew that no one in the Hill, no one, had ever seen the likes of it.

Suddenly he heard a noise. He cocked his ears, listening. Then he heard it again.

It came from the golden ball.

It was a tiny, chipping sound. The ball wiggled a bit, rocking slightly back and forth.

Twig's eyes widened as he saw a very small crack appear on the surface of the sphere. The crack grew larger.

Twig scurried behind a clump of weeds and peered back at the sphere. It shifted and jiggled some more, rocking more and tilting forward. Small sounds came from within it, peeps and clicks and whines, sounding like a combination of cries for help and growls of warning.

Twig was mesmerized. "Whatever it is," he whispered to himself, "it's hatching!"

chapter 7

A Dragon

T he shell split in half, the two pieces opening like a gooey, prehistoric flower bud, revealing a wiggling and slightly sticky creature unlike any that Twig had ever seen.

Twig didn't know what to think of the . . . what *was* it? It was covered with thousands of shiny, emerald-green scales. The scales rippled and shimmered, one moment flat against the curved back and round belly of the creature, then suddenly pointing out from its body, as though it was alarmed or excited.

A miniature mountain range of small, red-purple bumps ran down its spine, from the base of its head to the tip of its tail. It had two slightly rounded wings that looked as though they were made of soft, cinnamon-colored velvet, checkered with tiny veins of turquoise blue. A hooked claw jutted out at the crook of each wing, sharp and glinting in the sun.

Twig couldn't stop staring at its eyes. They were like two kaleidoscopes, fiery sunflower yellow, with flecks of brilliant gold and burnished copper. The tiny creature tilted its head this way and that, studying its surroundings for the first time.

It was formidable, but adorable. And Twig knew exactly where he had seen one before; it closely resembled the pictures in his book collection. It was a dragon.

Twig was fascinated, but cautious.

"W-w-well, hello, little guy," he ventured, his voice squeaky. "You're . . . real. You're not just a picture in a book!"

The dragon flicked its tail and

jerked its head
sideways, peering at
Twig. Its scales rippled.
"Are you looking for
your mommy?" Twig asked.

"Where's your momm . . . uh-oh?" He quickly spun around and looked in each direction.

The dragon stared at Twig for a moment, then opened its beak-like mouth.

"GRRRUUUK!"

Twig scooted back in surprise.

"GRRRRRUUUUUUK!" It flapped its velvety wings in rapid beats.

"Oh!" Twig exclaimed. "I guess I'm the mommy!"

"GRRRUUUUUK!" The dragon hopped at Twig, wings still fluttering, mouth agape, eyes excited and golden, almost landing on top of him.

"Whoa, not so fast, little fella. I'm just a temporary mommy."

There was a small cluster of wild grapes nearby; Twig hurriedly picked a few and laid them on the ground in front of the dragon baby, who sniffed at them with its tongue, as though experimenting, then looked up at Twig.

Twig was disappointed. "No?"

He thought for a moment, then took the grapes and squeezed them into a pulp.

"Better?"

The dragon sniffed again, then gobbled them down.

Twig lifted a small stone, finding a wriggling earthworm and a roly-poly bug, and made a presentation of them on a platter of bark.

"Here! How's this?"

The dragon let out a squeaky, plaintive bleat, like a rusty gate in a breeze, and then ate them up.

Twig tore leaves into strips and then chewed them a little and spit them out, thinking that perhaps mother dragons regurgitated when feeding their offspring. The dragon ate those, too.

"Good?" Twig asked.

The dragon squeaked again.

The fresh smell of wild cucumber was near. Twig located a tiny patch of the short, umbrella-like plant, one of his favorites. Digging down, he found his prize and wiped the dirt from the crispy white tuber.

Twig held out one of the roots, then took a bite himself, chewing noisily.

Scrunch . . . scrunch . . . scrunch.

Suddenly the tangle of ferns and wild cucumber plants exploded in a burst of wind and wings, and Twig felt what seemed like pins being dragged across his back. He squeaked and catapulted in a somersault.

The shiny black talons of a hawk had just barely grazed his back; the hawk had misjudged her distance by but a hair. A tiny bit closer and Twig would have been swinging in a death grip, talons slicing through his spine, as the hawk carried him through the understory of the forest.

Twig knew the hawk would, in the shake of a chipmunk's tail, return for a second attack. Quickly scanning the area, he saw a small pile of blue glass jars some distance away. Some lay with lids rusted tight; others were broken.

Wide-eyed, he turned to the dragon. "Quick!" he

exclaimed. "Let's go!"

The dragon looked at Twig blankly. In a panic Twig yanked at the dragon's tail to pull it along, and then grabbed hold of one of the dragon's wings. *"Now!"* he squealed, and then took off toward the broken jars. One was nearly covered with weeds and grasses. He darted to it, pushed the grasses aside, and pointed.

The dragon, as though this was a game, flapped and vibrated its tiny wings.

"In!" Twig squeaked at the dragon, pushing at its rear end. Twig immediately raced in behind, pulling grasses over the opening, and burrowed into the back of the jar.

Simultaneously they heard a loud *clink* as the hawk's talons hit the jar. The cloudy glass distorted the looming face, but Twig could see, just a whisker away, the eyes of the hungry hawk.

They were trapped.

The hawk glared into the jar. Twig knew that if it weren't for several millimeters of clear blue glass, the

hawk would eat him. The hawk shrieked again, furious and frustrated. Her beak was hard-edged and strong. She snapped at the jar, attacking repeatedly.

Now, with the yellow eyes of the hawk staring in, the dragon seemed to sense the danger. It backed against the curve of the glass, quivering.

"It's okay, buddy," Twig whispered. "I won't let anything happen to you."

They sat in the jar, Twig protectively covering the small dragon, until the hawk saw the futility of the situation, lifted her wings, and flew off.

Looking nervously at the sky, and heart still racing, Twig emerged from the jar, the dragon wiggling out after him. The fresh air outside was intoxicating, and Twig breathed in deeply. It felt good to be alive.

Now he suddenly wanted to be home. He looked at the dragon, his whiskers twitching. "Time for me to go," he said. "I'm heading back home now." He turned and started to scamper away, but the newly hatched dragon hopped after him.

"No, not with me," Twig ordered. "Head back home. Wherever that is."

The baby dragon blinked at Twig.

"Go home."

The dragon flicked its tail.

This time it was Twig who blinked. He knew he couldn't leave the defenseless creature alone in the Woods. But a dragon in the Hill? That wouldn't work. The Council would not have it.

Twig looked sympathetically at the dragon. He pondered. It would be difficult, but maybe if he *hid* the dragon . . . at least for a while . . .

He started home, the dragon scurrying behind. With the Naming Ceremony approaching, this was just what Twig needed: a hungry, homeless dragon.

chapter 8

A Hiding Place

Using the waning sun as his guide, Twig began to see familiar signs. He was getting close; the trees, the terrain, and the smells in the air were ones he recognized now. He rounded a large rock outcropping and saw the looming silhouette of the Yard in the distance.

He recognized a voice, some distance away. "Twig! Twig!"

"Lily?" he answered. "Over here!"

It had only been the best part of a day, but it was wonderful to hear a familiar voice, especially Lily's.

"Twig!" he heard again, closer this time.

He quickly pulled the baby dragon behind a tree stump. "Stay still!" he whispered. The dragon looked at him, cocking his head.

Just then Lily came scurrying up through the mayapples and toothwort.

"Where have you been?" she demanded. "You've been gone all day!"

"Sit down here for a minute," he said, leading Lily to the stump. He stood there for a moment and looked at her.

"All right, this is secret, right?" he said seriously. "No telling anyone, and I mean anyone!"

Lily's ears perked up, and she nodded. "Not a soul."

"This may be the most incredible, special thing you will ever see," he said proudly. "This may be th–"

Lily gasped impatiently. "What *is* it?"

Beaming, Twig half pulled, half pushed the baby dragon out from behind the stump.

The dragon lifted its head. "GRRUUUUK!"

Lily hopped
back. "Oh! Wow. That's
a—a—it's a—" she whispered.
"It's a dragon," Twig said.
Lily held out her paw, and the dragon stretched out
to sniff her. A snort of warm breath shot out.

"Ooh! He tickles!" she giggled. "Where did you find him?" The dragon's tail looped and flicked.

"I found his egg, in the dirt. Then I . . ." And Twig was off, telling Lily the whole story.

Lily smiled. "Have you named him yet?" she asked, gently stroking the dragon's snout and neck.

"He'll have to earn a name like the rest of us," Twig replied. "Something will come to us after he's settled in."

Lily choked. "Settled in?"

"He's just hatched. I can't abandon him."

"So you have a plan?"

"I'm sure I can hide him for a while, until I can train him a little, or at least until he can get along on his own. I don't want the rest of the Hill to know about him. I want to keep him as my secret." Twig looked at Lily. "*Our* secret."

Lily caressed the dragon's scales. "Where can you hide a baby dragon?"

"I was thinking: Why not the wooden clock tower near my house? Nobody ever goes there. It's empty. And I can lock him in so he can't get out."

Lily looked doubtful, but the dragon nuzzled her chin. "Well," she relented. "That might work. We can take turns bringing in food and keeping him company."

Twig smiled. "I notice you said 'we.'"

"Of course I said 'we.' For one thing, he's adorable. For another thing, he needs a home. And for another thing, you couldn't do this by yourself. We'll be his adoptive parents. Deal?"

"Deal!" replied Twig.

They set off through the mayapples toward the old clock tower, with the dragon trotting and flapping behind. The wooden tower was tilting and cloaked with weeds.

"It's creepier than I remembered," Lily said. The swollen door creaked as they brushed aside spiderwebs.

Inside, centipedes slithered into piles of dusty dead leaves.

But after spending some time cleaning up a bit, and letting fresh air in, they gently coaxed the dragon into its new home.

Twig found a stick and used it to hold the latch together. The dragon clawed at the door.

Lily tried cooing and reassuring it. "Do you think we can leave him without any problems?" she asked.

"We may have to come up with a plan B."

The two of them sat a little ways from the clock tower, listening to the dragon inside. They could tell it was anxious, pacing frantically around the inside of the dark space, making clicking and scraping noises. After a while the pacing stopped.

"I think he's okay now," Twig said. "We can check on him a little later."

"And bring him food," Lily remarked as they headed home. "Just your normal, everyday care of baby dragons."

They parted ways. The evening shadows were falling rapidly; Twig had been away for only the day, but so
much had happened.

Back at his burrow, Twig stepped into his kitchen.
Olive's elderberry pies had cooled.

A good ending to an eventful day.

chapter 9

A Sundial

After a few days Twig and Lily had developed a routine. They would meet surreptitiously at the clock tower between or after classes, letting the dragon explore and romp, and always being careful to go unnoticed.

The dragon flapped and fluttered its wings, like a baby bird fledging from its nest.

"His wings are so little . . . I wonder if he'll ever fly," Lily pondered.

"I bet they grow," Twig replied. "Why else would he have them?"

The two friends lounged on the leaves in the dappled sunlight, smiling as the dragon snorted and sniffed through the dry leaves, suddenly pouncing on an insect. He rummaged with his nose through the weeds and bumped headfirst into a rock.

Lily laughed. "He really is kind of a klutz," she said.

"Maybe even a bigger klutz than me," Twig added.

Lily looked up at the sun. Metal Crafting started promptly. "We'd better get to class," she said.

Twig sighed. It seemed like torture to have to leave the dragon, but they led it back to the clock tower and hurried down the path to school.

Class had nearly begun when they slid onto their bench seats.

"Attention, class," Professor Burdock said from the front of the room. A map of the Hill had been pulled down to conceal their next assignment. "Your next Metal Crafting project will be one that will be completed at home. It is a difficult one. Your skills will be tested to their limits. It will be more of a challenge to some"—he

looked straight at Twig—"than to others."

Twig burned under Burdock's gaze.

"Normally, at this point in the semester, I would want you each to design and construct a simple hinge. Sounds easy, but they are more difficult than you might think. However, for this next project, I have thought of something more unusual."

Twig wiggled uncomfortably. He was afraid to see what was under the map.

With a flourish, Master Burdock pulled at the map, and it shot up with a clatter.

USING FOUND MATERIALS, CONSTRUCT A SUNDIAL
OF YOUR OWN DESIGN THAT IS BOTH VISUALLY
APPEALING AND TELLS THE TIME OF DAY.
DUE IN ONE WEEK.

Twig gulped. A sundial? He had always told the time by the arch of the sun and didn't think much of how sundials were made. That would take some research. And a week wasn't very long.

After class Twig scampered through the school grounds and went directly to the Burrow of Records. In front of the entrance to the burrow sat an ancient sundial that he could use as a prototype. Already several other students had gathered, taking notes and sketching the sundial.

"Hey, Twig!" Sumac said as he approached. "Good luck with this one. . . . Remember, it's supposed to tell time, not explode in Professor Burdock's face!"

His pink mouse tail wiggled as he laughed, and the others chittered.

"Maybe Twig's sundial will only work at night!" another jeered.

The tips of Twig's ears turned red, but he tried not to notice the taunts. Instead he concentrated on the sundial. Moss and lichens decorated the carvings on the old marble pedestal. The broad face was a large disc made of copper, now green with time, as was the triangular gnomon. The gnomon cast a shadow on an arch of numbers, giving an indication of the time of day.

Twig studied the different parts of the sundial, already getting ideas of what to use from the piles of parts and pieces in his room. He raced home and then started to gather together his materials.

Spreading the things on the floor of his room, he

set to work, but his mind kept wandering back to the dragon. The thought of it sitting alone in the base of the clock tower kept gnawing at his conscience. *Who says I have to work on the sundial here?* he thought. Making sure no one was looking, he hauled everything out to the tower.

The next day he continued with his project near the clock tower, keeping a watchful eye on the dragon. He built a small fire and with difficulty tried his best at melting some solder to attach his parts together.

There were many stops and starts to getting the solder melted and trying to weld things together. It took several days and many attempts before Twig finally got the pieces attached. He felt fairly confident about the sundial design, and although it was a little fragile and lopsided, he was proud to have constructed it.

"Won't be the best in the class, but won't be the worst, either," he said, smiling at the dragon, putting everything in the tower and locking the door. He led the dragon back into the dark tower room. "Don't make any noise," he whispered to the dragon. "Be a good boy!"

Twig headed home.

chapter 10

Char

The next morning, Twig stared in disbelief.

The tower room was a mess.

The dragon had been alone and enclosed in the small space for too long. There were claw marks nearly everywhere, but especially at the door, where he had tried to dig or find his way out. Twig's work materials were scattered all over and had been trampled. But worst of all, his project was destroyed.

Twig picked up the pieces. He would have to start all over on the sundial. A sudden anger filled him head to toe, and he glared at the dragon. The dragon sensed Twig's mood and retreated to a corner, hunched and confused.

"You ruined it!" Twig squeaked, his anger swelling. "All that work for nothing! Why did you have to follow me home? Why did I find your egg?" With his paws clenched, he surveyed the broken mess, then curled on the floor, his head spinning.

The dragon, still cowering in the corner, made a coughing, raspy, deep-throated noise, a cough that caused its body to spasm. Twig sat up.

"You okay, boy?" he asked, suddenly feeling guilty about his angry outburst. He padded over to the corner. The dragon looked tired; it tucked its head beneath one wing. Twig reached out and stroked the dragon's smooth scales, scratching gently under its chin, speaking softly. "It's all right," he said. What had been rage was replaced with compassion. Ruining the sundial had been unintentional.

The dragon quivered at first, then relaxed. After a while, it stretched out its neck and closed its eyes.

Twig studied the mess that spread across the room. "Tomorrow I'll try to fix this," he said quietly.

The next morning, Twig set about trying to reassemble the sundial. His anger had gone, but he had lots of catching up to do if he was ever to make Master Metal Crafter. Lily stopped by, anxious to see the baby dragon, and saw Twig's project still strewn about the room.

Her tail wiggled anxiously. "What happened here?" she asked. "Although I can guess. Something tells me someone was a bad baby dragon. Oh, Twig . . . is it ruined?"

"Yes, ruined," Twig replied. "And you're correct . . . bad baby dragon is right."

"Professor Burdock is going to really going to be hard on you for this," Lily said soberly. She picked up one of the pieces. "Anything you can fix?"

Twig looked skeptical, ears drooped.

Lily went over to the dragon; it perked up and fluttered its wings when she approached. She couldn't help feeling bad for it, and stroked it gently.

"Are you all finished being a bad baby dragon?" she cooed.

"Good point," Twig said. "I know I won't be leaving any more of my projects here for him to mess up."

Lily kept scratching his throat. The dragon stretched out his neck, and his eyes rolled back in rapture.

"Hey, he really likes this," Lily whispered. "He's closed his eyes! He's so cute!"

Suddenly the dragon spasmed a bit and put his head low to the floor.

"He looks . . . weird," Twig said.

A moment later the dragon belched, and a short burst of flame shot from his nostrils.

"Oh!" shrieked Lily, bouncing back.

"Wow! Did you see *that?*" Twig cried out.

"All I did was stroke his chin a little. Then . . . kaboom!" Lily gasped.

They both stared at the dragon, who sat looking a little dazed. Thin curls of green-gray smoke curled from each nostril. The dragon snorted a bit, then blinked.

Twig nudged Lily. "Do it again," he urged.

"Do what again?"

"Rub his chin. Make him breathe flames again."

Lily looked at Twig and wiggled her whiskers. "You sure?"

"Yes! Go ahead! Or I'll do it. . . ."

Lily pushed at Twig. "I'll do it!" Again, she gently rubbed and scratched the dragon's throat and neck. "There, there," she murmured. The dragon stretched his neck out, this time with his eyes open, as though he wanted to see the fire again himself. After a minute, Lily got tired. "I don't think he's going to do it," she said. "Maybe he needs fuel?"

"Let me try," Twig suggested.

Lily scooted aside, and Twig began the scratch routine. This time the dragon immediately bent low; then, with a loud combination of snort, sneeze, and burp, shot another stream of fire out of his nose, much larger than the first. The flame shot across the room and scorched one wall. In a blinding flash, it was over.

Twig and Lily jumped back, falling backward and landing together in a heap. They looked at each other, amazed, and then started laughing.

"Wow!" Twig chittered.

"The flame!" Lily squealed. "He's a walking blowtorch!"

Twig pointed at a burned place in the wall, which smoked and popped. "Look at the wall . . . it's charred! He nearly burned the place down!" They looked at each other and started laughing again.

Lily sat upright. "That's it," she declared. "His name is Char! It can be short for Charcoal."

The dragon looked very pleased with himself. Again, his nostrils emitted curls of smoke, large curls this time, green-gray puffs that rose to the ceiling. His wings fluttered.

"Well, Char," Twig said. "You're quite a dragon."

Char looked at them, wings vibrating.

chapter 11

Practice

Twig started playing with fire. Char's fire, that is. He cajoled and scratched the little dragon, experimenting with the intensity and direction of the flame. At first, to get used to the novelty of using Char as a torch, he tried simple things like igniting a dried oak leaf.

Then the experimenting became more involved. By directing Char slightly, Twig discovered he could burn the letters of his name into a piece of wood. It took practice, but after many botched attempts, Twig figured out the exact right amount of stroking and scratching and encouraging, getting the correct heat, intensity, and amount of flame.

The little dragon was perfectly happy to oblige. He breathed out, long and slow. The flame was blue-white hot, capable of melting the hardest of metals and minerals. Miraculously, it didn't seem to affect Char's nose or mouth.

Lily stopped by to check on their progress. "Hey, Twig," she said, nuzzling Char, "have you thought about how Char could act as . . . uh . . . well, a bellows? And fire pit? All in one? He could maybe help you with your Metal Craft assignments. The homework ones, anyway."

"I beat you to it," Twig said. "Look what I already did." He held up two pieces of copper wire that had been melted together, crossed in the middle. "In half a second Char welded them. Perfectly. All I had to do was point him in the right direction and scratch him a little. And look here." Twig reached for an iron nail. It had been curled into an S shape. "Our next project. He heated the nail in the right place, right temperature, and I pounded the shape out. Perfect."

"I'm impressed," said Lily.

"There's more," said Twig.

He brought out another nail, this time pulled and twisted evenly, but pieces of copper wire had been heated and twisted with it. The dull iron and shiny copper swirled together into a metal ribbon. The result was a well-executed piece of Metal Craft.

"That's good! Even good enough for Professor Burdock," Lily remarked.

"I'm thinking I can do well enough, with my buddy here, to get my take-home assignments done. Maybe even well enough to earn Master."

111

"Maybe you're thinking a little ahead of yourself."

"Could be, but I've got some ideas. I'm ready for anything that Burdock can throw at me."

TWIG WAS ALREADY GETTING IDEAS OF WHAT TO USE FOR his new sundial, now that he had Char as an assistant. A whole new range of materials and parts had opened up. His room was full of things that would work; assembling them, however, had been another thing altogether. Now his projects could be bigger, fancier, and more elaborate. This would be delicate work; he hoped he could harness and direct Char's fire to weld the perfect sundial.

And Twig was noticing something else: the intricate pattern of Char's scales and the delicate veins in his wings were an inspiration. Char was a beautiful creature.

When he got home, he rummaged through the piles of pieces and parts, finally finding exactly what he knew would work. He gathered some of the pieces and then raced from the house, down the path toward the clock tower, anxious to make a fresh start on the assignment.

He was only about a five-minute scamper to the clock when, as he bounded over the roots of a giant oak, he heard a familiar voice.

"Going somewhere in a hurry, aren't we?"

Beau was sitting on one of the roots, paws clasped, as though he had been waiting for Twig. The look on his face was kind, but no-nonsense. He peered over his spectacles, his burly eyebrows raised.

"Well?" he asked. "Important engagement?"

Twig was sunk. Beau had that *I'm not in any hurry, this may take a while* manner. Char would be starving.

"I . . . uh, yes, Uncle Beau. I'm in sort of a kind of a hurry, I guess," he stammered.

"Mmm. Where to?" Beau asked.

"Uh, nowhere special." Twig gulped.

"With . . . what is that you have there? A clock piece? Anything you want to talk about, Twig?" the raccoon asked gently. "I mean, sometimes secrets can become burdens."

Twig looked a little uneasy. "I don't have any secrets. I mean burdens."

"No? Good. Because it isn't good if you find yourself going out of your way"—Beau glanced down the path—"to keep things from your friends or family."

"Um, yes, sir."

"You know, I remember once a long time ago when I was carrying around a burden, a terrible burden."

Twig's heart sank. He didn't have the time and wasn't in the mood for one of Beau's ancient stories.

"Really?" he said, edging a bit down the trail.

"Yes. I was about your age. I found something. Something very unusual. Very . . . special."

Twig stopped, suddenly interested and wary.

"I didn't tell a soul," the raccoon continued. "Not even my mother or father . . . afraid they'd think I was crazy. And you know what?"

"What, Uncle Beau?"

"I never did tell anyone. Ever. I still have the secret."

"Really? You never told?"

"Nope. I've kept it to myself for nearly an eagle's age. And you know what else?"

"What?"

"Wish I had. Wish I'd told somebody. At least then I would have had the burden off me. A secret isn't worth much if you can't share it. 'Course, that doesn't make it very much of a secret, if you tell. But it's sort of like a cherry turnover. If you share it with somebody, it's a lot more delicious."

Twig stood there, thinking. He was glad to be able to share his secret with Lily.

"Nothing is tougher than being untrue to yourself, Twig, or to others. Sometimes keeping a secret can get you into trouble."

Twig looked down. He pondered telling Beau about Char. He decided he wasn't ready. "Thanks, Uncle Beau," he said finally. "I'll keep what you said in mind. I need to go. Bye!"

And he dashed away.

He and Char had a project to do.

chapter 12

Becoming Masterful

Twig needed a more secluded spot to work, way out in the Woods, not on anyone's main pathway. He chose a clearing under some alder saplings and used a small cart to secretly bring all his supplies and materials to his workspace under the alders.

"Now listen carefully, Char," he said to the dragon. "I put the pieces in place, you melt the metal to hold them together, just like we've practiced before, okay?"

Char looked at Twig and blinked. His tongue flicked out. Twig smiled. "Let's get warmed up."

Twig touched a length of lead solder to the two pieces of scrap metal, while Char spit flame, melting the solder. The two pieces held perfectly. The soldering, though rough and sloppy-looking at first, was fairly professional by the time they had finished. It was neatly and evenly laid, not too much solder and not too little. Twig even added a flourish at the end, producing a small solder curlicue.

He looked proudly at the piece of metalwork.

"Char, we're a team!" he announced. "If this is how we start off, imagine how good we'll do after more practicing!" He gave Char a gentle stroke on his chin. A little puff of smoke came out of the dragon's nostrils, and he closed his eyes in rapture.

Twig got back to work. He pushed and pulled a pewter sugar bowl into the middle of the clearing.

"Okay, Char. Here is your first real test. I want a nice, clean cut all around, straight and even. Now let's see some flame!"

Twig patted Char on the neck, making coaxing

sounds, and Char snorted, abruptly producing a blue-white flame that burst out and hit the pewter with a spitting sizzle.

"Whoa! Too much, Char," Twig said. "Easy does it."

Char seemed to sense Twig's directions, and with another snort, a smaller, more directed flame shot from his throat.

"Good boy!" Twig smiled. With very slight shifts in pressure, he was able to control Char's flame, both in strength and direction. "Good boy!" Twig said again, slowly, slowly turning the bowl as Char breathed his fire. A melted line separated the top of the bowl from the bottom, and in several minutes the top teetered away, landing in the dirt.

Twig examined the melted edge. It was perfectly smooth and even. "It sparkles!" he marveled. "So shiny . . . and glittery!" He looked at Char. "This would have taken me days to do. And it wouldn't have looked so . . . special." He gave the dragon a hug around his neck. "Thank you, Char."

The success of the sliced sugar bowl excited Twig. Suddenly Master Metal Crafter didn't seem so far-fetched.

They spent the rest of the afternoon at work, using a fancy metal fish fin handle for the gnomon of the sundial. Twig used old copper wire to hold it in place, and used the wire to create a pattern of bends and curls. The copper, newly melted, glistened shiny and bright. Twig cut more copper wire into tiny pieces, using smaller gauge. He bent them into numbers with flourishes and twists. Char's intensely hot flame melted them into place.

The sundial face became a beauti-ful, copper-rich

design that amazed and delighted Twig.

A damselfly landed on Char's nose and sat there in the sun. Twig watched it for a moment, and then got an idea. He twisted thin silver wire into an insect motif, laying the pieces around the lip of the sundial platform. He then added tiny flecks of gold in the wings, pieces that he had found and accumulated from discarded electronics. The sundial, with its gold, silver, and copper burnished by Char's intense blue-hot flame, and with Twig's delicate artistic touch, was a thing of beauty.

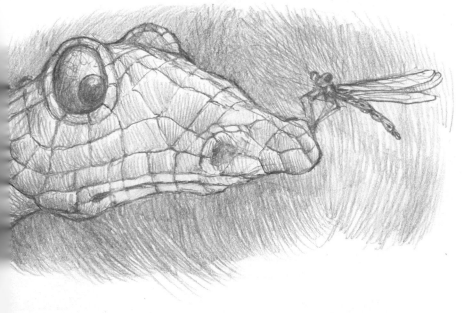

Twig stood back, contented. Proud.

"Burdock won't believe we did this!" he said. "Nobody will. Thank you, buddy. You . . . you inspire me!" He gave Char another squeeze, holding him tightly. Char rippled his scales, and puffs of gray smoke came out of his nostrils. Twig held the dragon's face.

"You look tired, Char," he said. "Let's get you back home. You need some rest after all that."

Twig dragged several fern fronds over to the sundial, piling and arranging them until his new project was camouflaged and hidden from view.

"No one would ever know it was here," he said to himself, pleased.

They set off through the Woods. Twig's whiskers twitched with anticipation.

SHORTLY AFTER DAWN TWIG, WITH LILY IN TOW, SCAMpered through the Woods to the hidden clearing.

"What is going on?" Lily asked repeatedly. Even though slightly irritated at being summoned at an early

124

hour, and then traipsing into the Woods, Lily was a bit excited; she knew Twig must have a good secret to share. They rounded a bend, and then Twig led her off the trail to the ferns. "Ready?" he asked, beaming.

"I've been ready for the last half hour," Lily sighed.

"Okay! Presenting . . . my sundial project!" he squealed, pulling away several of the fronds to reveal the newly made sundial. Rays of sunlight filtered through the forest canopy, illuminating the sundial, the bright light hitting the polished metals. It glowed. Lily sat back onto the ground, eyes wide in amazement.

"Oh!" she gasped. She sniffed around the sundial, examining every inch, her whiskers quivering.

"But Twig . . . the detail . . . the craftsmanship. Did you make this? No offense." Lily looked squarely at him. "Help from Char?"

"Char did help . . . a little," Twig admitted.

Lily's ears twitched and wiggled. "Twig, it's awesome," she gushed. "It's sure to be the best in the class."

"Thanks, Lily. We've got to get it back to school. You get one side, I'll get the other."

They heaved and lifted, getting the sundial safely tied onto the cart, and then headed through the Woods to the Hill. Several teachers were arriving for classes as were students with their projects. They all stared in awe as the cart was pushed into the school entrance courtyard. A crowd gathered, everyone guessing it was Lily's sundial project.

"Nope," she said. "Not me!" She gestured at Twig.

"Did you help him, Lily?" said Hyacinth, looking suspicious. "You know that is against the rules."

"Nope. Didn't lift a paw," Lily replied.

Twig was beaming, his whiskers twitching with pride.

Everyone's tone had changed.

"Hey . . . great job, Twig," Anemone said.

"Yeah, Twig, good work," commented Finch.

Just then Professor Burdock arrived. He looked slightly confused, seeing Twig standing next to a beautiful work of metal art. The sundial gleamed, almost magically. He padded up to the cart. His paw lightly touched the rim of the sundial, then glided along the glittering filigreed metals, tracing each curl and tendril, the wings of the metallic bee.

"Whose work is this?" he asked.

"It's Twig's," Ivy answered.

Burdock looked at Twig, who nodded.

"Quite extraordinary," the weasel murmured, with no attempt to hide his surprise. "Yes, quite extraordinary."

Professor Amaranth and Professor Fern walked by the courtyard and saw the commotion.

"Oh, my!" cooed Professor Amaranth, a Master Glassblower. "Very nice welding. Very nice! Whose project is this?" She looked at Lily. "Yours?"

"It's . . . it's Twig's," Burdock answered reluctantly.

"At least he says it's his. Even and smooth, not too heavy, not too light. The soldering is just right. And the precious metals decorative work is a beautiful touch," he said. "It glitters!"

"Thank you," Twig said sheepishly.

Burdock glared at Twig. "And you . . . ahem . . . had no help with this project?" he queried.

Twig glanced around. "Um . . . no, sir."

The Metal Craft teacher could not resist touching the smooth, shiny metal rim again.

Twig's classmates looked at one another, amazed. Twig smiled whisker to whisker.

chapter 13

The Necklace

Twig scurried into the house.

"Well!" said his mother, coming from the kitchen, drying her paws. "How was your day?"

"I just turned in my Metal Craft project," Twig replied. He found himself turning red at the ears. "It's . . . pretty good."

"Oh?" his mother exclaimed. "Funny. You never liked Metal Craft before. Now you can hardly wait to get to class. But your take-home assignments . . . I never see you working on them."

"I . . . I do lot of them at school, in my free time. Or over at Lily's," Twig answered. He felt his fur ripple nervously. "I like working on them when no one is around, so I wait until after school sometimes."

"Hmm," said Olive. "Well, anyway, I've invited Beau over for dinner tonight." She was spreading a brightly flowered cloth over the oak table, smoothing it out, and placing a vase of honeysuckle flowers in the center. "Get washed up. He'll be here soon."

"What are we having?" called Twig from his washbasin.

"Artichokes!" Olive called back.

That explained the delicious smells: artichokes stuffed with garlic, pine nuts, spices, and morels, and stewed pawpaws, and deep-dish elderberry pie with maple-seed custard sauce. Twig's mouth watered.

There was a knock and then a familiar voice.

"Halloo! Your guest has arrived," Beau hollered as he hobbled into the house, his gait stiff and slow. The kitchen glowed with the warmth of good food being prepared.

Twig smiled and greeted the elderly raccoon with a paw shake. "Hi, Beau," he said. "Mom's made some of your favorites."

"Ah . . . is that elderberry pie I smell?"

"Everything's ready!" Olive sang out from the kitchen. "Beau, have a seat."

"Thank you," Beau said gratefully, sitting down at his place of honor on the carved bench.

Olive's steamed artichoke dish filled the air with its savory aroma, and Twig took note of the elderberry pie, still warm, waiting to be sliced, bursting with its juicy dark-purple berries.

Beau gave Twig a glance. "So, Twig," he said, carefully spreading a checkered napkin on his lap. "Tell me about your classes. How is school going?"

"Pretty good, I guess," Twig answered.

Beau took a large spoon and began to serve up the plump artichokes. Satiny gravy coated the chunks of morels and wild onions as he spooned a hefty portion onto Twig's plate.

"Just pretty good?" Beau asked. "I hear it's much better than just pretty good."

Twig grinned.

"As I heard it, you created quite a stir with your Metal Craft assignment. Professor Amaranth saw it and told me. Your sundial was the buzz of the school."

Olive looked at her son. "Twig? What's all this about?

You made something outstanding in Metal Craft?"

Twig blushed.

Beau continued. "Outstanding, is what I heard," he said. "The best take-home assignment they've seen in years."

"Take-home?" Olive asked. She studied Twig carefully. Twig was blowing on his food, cooling it, pretending not to notice the stares. "Twig?"

"I did the assignment . . . outside," he explained. "I wanted . . . privacy."

"Outside? Where?" Olive asked.

"Out in the Woods."

Olive looked at him suspiciously. "You built a fire? You had your equipment with you? You took all your tools?"

Twig stirred his food, smiling. "I had everything I needed," he said proudly.

Beau arched his thick eyebrows as he spoke. "Someday you'll have to tell me the secret of your success, Twig," he said.

Twig devoured his dinner. The artichokes were even tastier than usual.

ALTHOUGH TWIG'S CLASSROOM WORK OFTEN STILL ENDED badly—Professor Burdock called him "Woodpecker Toes" one day after he fumbled with some molten solder and burned a hole in the worktable—it was definitely improving. The delicacy of the work and his use of more complicated metal combinations became the talk of the school. All the novices and intermediates came to admire his projects. The accolades made Twig think that maybe he had a chance at becoming Twig Metal Crafter after all.

But with the accolades also came rising suspicion. Classmates whispered about the fact that Twig only truly excelled at take-home work, and that the classroom assignments were less successful. The scrutiny only made Twig more nervous under the watchful eyes of his professors.

Basil was particularly annoyed with Twig's successes and was determined to get to the bottom of the mystery. He had quickly gone from "head of the class" to "second rate" in Metal Craft, and it infuriated him to watch Twig basking in praise. He clenched his paws so tightly that he felt his claws stabbing into his pads.

A few days later, Twig hurried to the tower, carrying a variety of practice supplies, and then headed with Char to their hidden workplace. After welding a series of straight pins into a filigreed necklace, the two relaxed in the late-day sun.

Twig smiled, holding up the delicate silver jewelry. "I may take this home to Mom. She'd think I did it in class." He thought about the pleasure he'd have giving it to Olive.

But there was also a guilty feeling. He hadn't done it on his own. And he would definitely lose his chance of being Named if anyone found out about the help he'd had making it.

There was a rustling in the leaves down the slope. Twig hopped quietly onto a log. Up the hill, through the toothwort and wild ginger, came Professor Burdock.

"Oh gosh . . . what is *he* doing here?" whispered Twig. He tried to decide what to do next. Burdock was heading directly through the little sunlit clearing. Twig turned and jumped behind the log. He quickly pulled the dragon beside him, camouflaging him with sticks and leaves. Char sat, blinking.

Burdock padded into the clearing. Suddenly, he stopped. Twig watched as the weasel jerked his head and then looked closely at the ground. He had spotted something. Twig followed his eyes; he saw a tiny glint of silver in the leaves. The necklace.

Burdock bent to pick up the necklace, examining it carefully. He looked around, sensing someone near. His tail flicked and twitched.

"Hello?" he said. "Who's there?"

He stood silent and motionless for a moment.

An emerald-colored bee droned into the clearing, then darted off.

Burdock paused a moment more, then, draping the necklace over his shoulder, disappeared down the narrow path.

chapter 14

Suspension

The next day at Metal Craft, end-of-semester home-work assignments came trickling in. Professor Burdock had all the students' projects on display on the front table.

Hyacinth brought in a trivet, made from old machin-ery parts, fairly well made, but definitely nothing to be excited about. "It lacks . . . imagination," Burdock said. "Functional, but not inspired."

Lily brought in a picture frame. Everyone giggled when she placed it on the display table, for it held a drawing that she had made of herself. The frame, of twisted clothes hangers that had been heated and melted into a pattern, looked like woven metal.

"Delightful," Burdock cooed. "Lightweight . . . interesting designs. Nice job, Lily." Lily reddened and looked embarrassed, suddenly wishing she had chosen another picture to put in it.

Basil's project was a copper-and-brass water dipper, made from an old perfume bottle cap. It had an elaborate handle that ended with a flourish, wrapped around a decorative coin.

"Very nice, Basil, very nice," said Burdock. "Commendable workmanship."

Several other students showed their creations—a door handle, a wall lighting sconce, a matching spoon, fork, and knife set—all very nicely made, but nothing spectacular.

Twig was last. He had designed a fireplace poker, with filigreed design work of ferns and acorns. He laid the poker on the display table. Burdock's eyebrows arched in a smile. The poker, although simple in that it was just a length of wrought iron, was almost a work of art. It was just the right length and weight. The handle was smooth to hold in a comfortable grip. The poker had all the marks of a well-crafted utilitarian object.

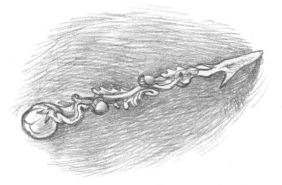

But in addition, a beautiful design of oak leaves and acorns wound up the length of the handle, delicate and detailed. Twig had used very thin silver wire for the intricate decoration, the silver leaves accented with copper acorns. At the end of the handle was a large ball bearing held firmly in place, shiny and perfect. A brass "T" was inlaid in the ball.

Burdock looked at Twig. "Excellent work," he said. "You should be very proud of yourself. Not only is the craftsmanship excellent, but the design and artistry are as well."

Lily beamed.

Basil glowered in disgust. "Twig does something right for a change," he whispered to Finch. "And suddenly everybody is saying how great he is."

"You're just jealous," Finch whispered back.

"I'm not jealous!" Basil grumbled. "It's just weird, that's all. All of a sudden, he's good at Metal Craft. And I'm going to figure out why."

Professor Burdock had sauntered to the front of the room. "I applaud everyone for excellent work on your assignments," he said, slowly gliding along the table. "Grades for these will be posted tomorrow."

He stopped to examine the fire poker again, his paws feeling up and down the smooth, filigreed decorations. A smile crept slowly across his face, and he gently laid the poker back on the table.

"Meanwhile, we begin discussion of our last topic: Unusual Metals and their Properties." The weasel began the classroom lecture, slowly circling his desk, until finally he stopped, opened a drawer, and withdrew from it a silver chain necklace, made from straight pins.

No one seemed to pay much attention, except Twig, who let out a tiny squeak. Burdock glanced at Twig and, smiling a bit more, continued his lecture. As he spoke, he placed the delicate chain around his neck, then passed among students' desks, lecturing all the while.

Twig squirmed in his seat. He was too nervous to pay attention to the lecture. The similarities in the craftsmanship of the necklace and the fireplace poker had not gone unnoticed by Professor Burdock. He stopped beside Twig's desk and turned toward him.

Twig looked up at the Master Metal Crafter. He was gazing down at Twig with an unpleasant grin. He was playing with the necklace, turning and twisting it between his paw pads. "Well, Twig," he said. "Notice anything? My necklace?"

"It's very nice, Professor Burdock," Twig replied with a gulp.

"I should say so. I would also say that you know who made it!"

Twig gulped again.

Burdock turned to glare at Lily. "You know who made it, too, don't you? In fact, it *was* you. Conniving with Twig on his take-home assignments." He looked at Twig again. "The two of you are in big, big trouble."

"Professor Burdock, I di—" Lily began, but Burdock wasn't listening. He leaned over Twig. "This is just the kind of behavior I would expect from you. Just like your father. Using someone else to do your work, and taking the credit!"

At the mention of his father, Twig had found his voice. "Professor Burdock," he said. "You are correct. The necklace is mine."

"Aha!"

Twig's tone was defiant. "But you are wrong about Lily. She did not help me make it. And she didn't help me with any of my other projects, either."

"Ha! I've seen the way the two of you are always whispering and plotting. There is no way you could have made these things without her help."

"She did not help me!"

"She not only helped you, but she's lying to protect you from being found out as a cheat!"

Twig felt the anger inside him reach the tip of his ears. "Saying I did something I didn't do is just as bad as lying or cheating!" he said.

"How dare you speak to me that way," Burdock growled. "You are dismissed. And suspended for today and tomorrow. Leave! Now!"

chapter 15

Advice from Uncle Beau

Twig sat on a stone, poking the ground with a stick, waiting for Lily to finish class. Finally he saw her leave the classroom, glance around, and then spot him through the mayapples.

She looked at him worriedly. "Wow," she said solemnly. "I don't ever remember seeing Burdock that angry. How was your mom about it? Have you told her yet?"

"Not yet. Dreading it," Twig replied.

They got up and walked in silence for a bit.

"I think Char is so amazing," Lily said, trying to

change the subject. "I mean, he's a dragon! You have a pet dragon!"

"Well, it's amazing, but look what trouble I've gotten into," Twig said. "I've been kicked out of class . . . twice. Everyone thinks I'm a cheat."

An enormous tiger swallowtail flew across the path in front of them, and they stopped to watch.

"You know, Twig, that no matter what, we're friends. I couldn't believe how you stood up for me today. Burdock's eyes really bugged out!"

"I know," said Twig. "For a second I thought his whiskers were going to ignite!"

They both giggled.

"Thanks, Lily," he said. "It's nice having you there." They came to the main path.

"Which way?" Lily asked.

Twig considered the trail for a moment. "I'm going to stop by and see Beau," he said. "I know it'll make me crazy if I don't talk to him and try to explain. See you tomorrow?"

"See you tomorrow. Good luck, Twig."

A little nervous, Twig headed off to Beau's cottage. He tugged at the doorbell chain three times, his signal.

"Ah, my friend Twig," Beau said genially as he opened the door. "I won't fib and say you're unexpected. Come in, my boy." He shuffled into the kitchen. "I just happened to be sitting down to some sassafras tea," the raccoon said. "Could I interest you in a cup?"

"Thanks, Beau." Twig noticed that the kitchen table was set for two, and the kettle was already boiling.

"Sit, sit," Beau said, grabbing a threadbare pot holder. He poured the scalding-hot water into the two mismatched cups, a freshly cut piece of sassafras root in each.

The spicy scent of sassafras filled the kitchen. It was one of Twig's favorites. Beau took his seat at the table.

"Ah," he sighed, sipping the hot tea carefully. "That hits the spot."

"Mm," Twig agreed, peering over his cup.

Beau pushed a bowl of shelled walnuts across the table. "Help yourself," he said. But then his eyes became serious. "Twig, you shouldn't have spoken like that to Master Burdock."

Twig figured that word had already gotten around about his outburst in class that afternoon. "I know," he replied. "I'm sorry. Really sorry."

"It's Master Burdock you'll need to apologize to.

You know, Twig, you'll have to control your temper better if you want to become a Master Metal Crafter."

"Do you think I ever will be one?" Twig asked quietly.

"I've never been good at making predictions, Twig, and don't want to try now. Do you *want* to be one?"

"I thought I did, but now . . . it feels good to do well, but it's not what I want to be, Beau."

"What do you want to be?"

"I'm not sure yet."

"I don't know if you'll become a Master Metal Crafter, or what. No one can say. But I will tell you this, Twig. You've got a fine head on your shoulders. And a big heart. . . . That counts for a lot. Maybe there are bigger and better things out there besides metalworking. I see in you someone who is destined for great things. You'll find your way, if you're true to yourself."

"How do you know if you're being true to yourself?" Twig asked.

"You'll know. You'll feel it."

Twig sat in silence for a moment, sipping the delicious tea. His mind was on more important things than Metal Craft.

"Beau," he said hesitantly, staring into his cup. "What do you know about . . . dragons?"

Beau's eyebrows went up. "Dragons? What do you mean, 'dragons'?"

"Dragons," Twig continued. "You know, like in my picture books. Do you think they exist?"

"Well, now . . . that's a peculiar question. But yes, I think they really exist. I heard stories about them, when I was little."

Twig sat up. "Like what?"

"I remember a story I heard a long, long time ago, from an ancient badger. I was just a youngster. You think I'm old? This badger was so old he could remember the first computer that was discovered at the Hill."

Twig's eyes widened. "Wow," he murmured.

Beau continued, "I remember him saying that *he* remembered somebody who had actually *seen* a dragon. Now keep in mind, this is a long-ago memory from someone who had a long-ago memory. But I can still recall how the old badger lit up like a firefly as he told the story. Of how the dragon had emerald-green scales, and beautiful wings. And he said the dragon had been discovered in the Woods, not far from here, and that it had been so startled at being seen it flew off, fast, through the trees."

"It flew?" asked Twig.

"Yep. That's what he said. Good flier, too, from the sound of it, dodging the trees and branches and going fast. Pretty amazing, eh?"

Twig took a sip of his tea. "Yeah . . . amazing," he said.

Beau poured a little more hot water over his sassafras roots. "Tell me, Twig," he said evenly, looking across his teacup. "What would you do if you ran across a dragon in the Woods?"

"Me? Oh, I—uh—I—" Twig stammered.

"Would you . . . run?" Beau prompted.

"No. I mean, I don't guess I would," Twig replied.

"Would you hide?"

"No, not that either, I don't think. . . ."

Beau looked at Twig steadily. "Would you try to capture it?" he asked.

Twig gulped his tea, glancing at Beau. The old raccoon gazed over his spectacles.

"Well," Twig finally answered. "Maybe. I think I'd try to find out if he was dangerous or not. Then I . . . maybe I'd try to bring him home."

"Interesting," Beau said.

Twig's head was swimming with all sorts of thoughts, but he was afraid that he was being cornered. "I should go now," he said.

Beau looked at him squarely. "Anything you want to share with me, Twig?"

"No . . . I'm good."

"Well, just tell me one thing. That you'll never say anything but the truth to me, always."

"I promise, Beau."

"Finished your tea?"

Twig took one last gulp. "Yes."

"Then off you go. Your mom will be getting worried."

Beau gave Twig a reassuring pat on the back and sent him on his way.

chapter 16

Olive

Twig plodded slowly up the pathway. He could hear the sound of hammer on chisel and knew his mother was busy with her sculpture. It was a bit of a relief; maybe she'd be less inclined to ask about his day.

Not this day.

"Twig? That you?" she called out from her work-room.

"Hi, Mom," Twig said with a bright chirp, trying to sound at ease.

"What happened at school today?" she asked,

chipping delicately at a piece of marble.

Twig watched her work for a moment. "Oh, nothing," he answered.

"How's Lily?"

"She's good."

"How were classes?"

Twig hesitated. "Okay, I guess."

Olive cocked her soft ears. "Just okay?"

"Pretty good."

His mother was unrelenting. "Twig . . . is there something you want to tell me?"

"Uh . . . no. In fact, there's something I'm trying pretty hard not to tell you."

Olive stopped her work and turned toward him. "What is it?"

Twig sighed, thinking he might as well get it over with. "Professor Burdock kicked me out of school today."

Olive put down her chisel. "He did *what?*"

"He suspended me. For today and tomorrow."

"For what? What did you do?"

"Mom," Twig moaned.

"Tell me what you did before I go to see Professor Burdock myself and ask him face-to-face!"

"I . . . I guess you'd say I back-talked." Twig rolled his eyes, body slumped, waiting for her reaction. It came quickly.

Olive stared at Twig in disbelief, her tail quivering. "Please tell me you are joking," she said.

Twig related the whole classroom incident. Olive looked at her son for a minute, then picked up her chisel and begin chipping again at the marble. "Well, I'm angry with you for being suspended, Twig," she said. "But I admire your ability to stand up for Lily."

"I didn't mind getting yelled at myself nearly as much as I minded him yelling at Lily."

Olive's brown eyes softened. "I know. Sometimes it's easier to feel pain yourself than to imagine others having to feel it."

Twig looked at her gratefully. "Well, anyway," he continued, "I told Burdock that he shouldn't talk to Lily that way and, well, he ordered me out. He was plenty mad."

"But I bet Lily was tickled that you defended her," Olive added with a smile. "Please tell me . . . she was *there*, wasn't she?"

"Yeah." Twig grinned. "She heard everything."

"Well, that's good, at least," Olive sighed. "We'll talk more about this some other time, if you want.

Wash your paws for dinner. And I made mashed cricket pudding."

LATER, TWIG CREPT QUIETLY OUT OF THE HOUSE. IT WAS dark as pitch, but he couldn't sleep. Too much had happened during the day for him to shut his mind off and get some rest. He wanted to see Char.

All was quiet at the wooden tower, Twig was relieved to see. But as soon as he approached, he heard clawing at the door.

Twig slipped inside. Char vibrated his wings, and the pink-and-yellow tongue slithered this way and that in greeting. Even though Char wasn't his usual rambunctious self, his eagerness at seeing Twig made the chipmunk smile.

"Hey, Char!" Twig cooed.

He sat with the dragon for a long while, scratching his chin, stroking his velvety wings. But even in the dark of the tower room Twig could see his bright colors had faded. Char looked tired. His scales seemed irregular, and his skin sagged.

Soon Char dozed off. Twig grinned as the dragon jerked in his sleep, kicking and wiggling his feet, possibly because of a dream, then tucked his head under his wing. The familiar snoring began, and Twig quietly tiptoed out, carefully latching the door, and scampered down the path.

Not a breath of breeze was stirring, and the air was sweet and dewy, full of the scent of locust blossoms. The moon was like a thin slice of crabapple, and Twig could see stars far above him between clumps of the Woods canopy. He silently made his way home under the umbrella-like mayapples—owls were a constant danger—and then tiptoed into the house and up to his room. Olive was still busy with her sculpture. She did not say a word, and Twig wondered if she had known he was gone the whole time.

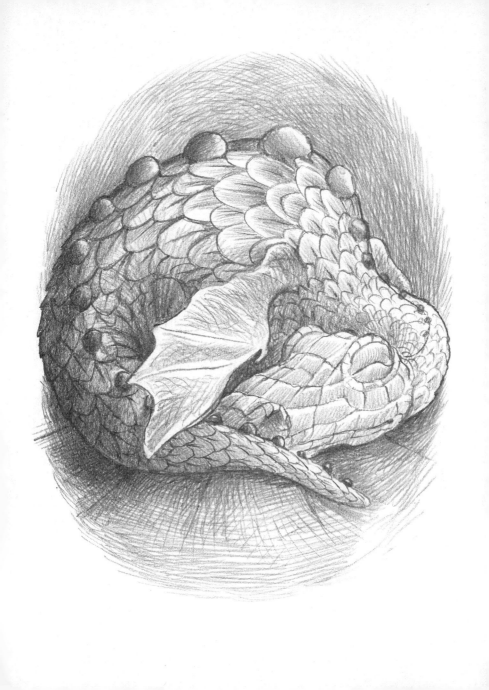

chapter 17

Basil

Twig decided to create one final masterpiece. It wasn't for school; it wasn't for credit. It was for fun.

And when he was finished, it was spectacular: a wind catcher. It wasn't anything useful, yet it was amazing. It whirred and chimed and clicked, but it didn't have any purpose except to catch the breeze. It was made from dozens of the parts and pieces that had littered Twig's bedroom. And it glittered and glowed under the burnished handiwork of Char's flame.

Twig gave a few spots a final polish. He stepped

back, admiring the brass-and-copper piece, and his foot landed on Char's tail. The dragon flinched slightly, but otherwise didn't move.

"Sorry, Char," Twig said absently, and then stopped. "Char . . . you okay?"

Char was noticeably thinner than he had been several weeks earlier. His emerald-green scales were now gray and dull. They didn't ripple with excitement. Twig noticed that even Char's eyes were funny. Filmy and lackluster, they were not the shiny gold they had been.

"We'll have some fun today, Char!" Twig said brightly. For a second he wondered if his cheery tone was for Char or for himself. He knew Char didn't belong inside the old tower.

"You'll be okay, Char. You just need some rest," said Twig.

The dragon lifted his head and blinked.

TWIG HURRIED BACK ALONG THE PATH, UNDER THE MAY-apples, carrying a sack full of spicebush berries. His mother would be making a spicebush berry cake this evening, Twig thought, or maybe spice acorn pudding. His mouth began to water.

"Where are you going so fast?" came a voice from directly up the path, and Basil appeared, blocking his way.

Twig tried to scoot by. "I've got no time for you, Basil."

"Oh yeah?" Basil replied. He reached into Twig's bag uninvited, pulled out a ripe berry, and began to munch. "You better make some time for me, 'cause I've got an important message for you."

Twig looked doubtful. "Important message? From?"

"From Professor Filbert. He's at school. I think he wants to tell you how good you're doing in class or something stupid like that. He said to make sure I found you, and to make sure you come see him."

Twig squinted at Basil suspiciously. "Why'd he ask me to come to him? Why can't he just see me tomorrow at school?"

"How should I know?" Basil replied, sounding annoyed.

Basil scampered off but stopped just past a bend in the path to look back at Twig. Twig was still pondering what to do. In a moment, with a glance at the pathway home, he started off down the forked trail, down to the school.

TWIG GOT TO THE SCHOOL AND SCAMPERED TO THE Electricity Lab. Professor Filbert was at his desk, a tall, elderly rabbit, missing patches of brown fur here and there from electrical burns. He pushed his spectacles up on his nose as he peered through them at Twig.

"Ah!" he chirruped. "Just in time." He fumbled with stacks of papers on his desk. "I'm sure you wouldn't mind helping me, would you, Twig, my boy? Hard to manage, you see. Lots of homework papers to grade tonight. Thank you so much."

"Uh, well, you see . . . ," Twig began. But the professor had already dumped the large pile of homework into Twig's arms and was absent- mindedly hopping out of the classroom.

"Keep up, my boy!"

Professor Filbert called back to Twig, who scurried after him, trying to keep the stack of papers in his arms. They took a circuitous route to the professor's burrow, a cozy but tangled labyrinth of tunnels beneath an old, rusty wheelbarrow.

"You can set the papers there, my boy. Excellent! Thank you so much! Could never have made it home by myself. Lucky you came along!" he squeaked. "Now, how about a cup of blackberry tea as a thank-you?"

Twig had the sinking realization that coming to see Professor Filbert was just a ruse that Basil had concocted. He wasn't sure why, but he wanted to find out, and find out immediately.

"Uh, no thank you, sir," he said. "I have to get home right away. Uh . . . my mom ordered me to."

"Well, can't disobey a mother's orders, eh?" the old rabbit chuckled. "Off you go. Be quick. Can't thank you enough."

Twig darted off to the tower, his heart pounding.

176

Basil suspected something. And if he found out about Char, so would Burdock. He hated to think of what they might do to Char.

He raced faster.

Twig got to the clock tower. He saw Basil surveying the scene, and then, creeping alongside the clock, peeking into cracks. He started to push open the door.

"Basil!" Twig yelled out. "What are you doing here?"

"I'm going to find out what your big secret is," he said. "Everybody knows your projects were done by someone else, and I'm going to find out who. All I had to do was follow Lily. Easy as pie."

Just then Lily poked her head out the tower door. "Go away, Basil!" she squeaked, pushing at Basil. She yanked on his whiskers. "Don't come in here!" Twig pulled on his tail.

"Ouch! Let go, you maniacs!" he yelled back,

shoving past Lily. His eyes grew large as they became accustomed to the dark of the tower's interior. In the dim light he could just make out what he thought was a pile of dead leaves, but it moved.

"Hello?" he said nervously. His fur stood on end as the shape quivered, and then two wings started to flutter.

"H-hey . . . ," he stuttered. He heard a popping sound. Then came a small flash of light as Char burped a warning flame, lighting the corner.

"Whoa!" Basil shrieked, eyes wide as he saw Char. He scrambled backward, falling through the door and out into the leaves outside. Twig slammed the door shut with a bang.

"What was *that*?" Basil exclaimed, panting heavily.

"I told you not to go in there!" Lily squeaked harshly.

"Now you know, Basil," fumed Twig. "You can't say anything to anybody. You can't!"

Basil was still shaking but was beginning to put two and two together. Suddenly he smiled. "It's all making sense now," he said. "Sure! Twig wasn't so hot at Metal Craft before . . . but now he is." He slapped his paws together. "Wait until Uncle Burdock hears about this!" he said, and darted off into the weeds.

"What? No, Basil!" Twig called out after him. "You can't tell a soul!"

But Basil had disappeared into the greens of the forest floor, heading to his uncle Burdock's house.

chapter 18

Char, Unleashed

In no time, Basil and his uncle arrived back at the clock tower, Burdock with a coil of rope in his paws. Lily steamed with anger.

"He's just a baby!" she called out. "Don't hurt him!"

Char lay tense and shaking in his corner. The dragon's scales were grayish and pointing awkwardly from his body. The weasel and his nephew approached slowly.

Burdock eyed the dragon with awe, but suspiciously. "A dragon," he said. "So they do exist. And you were using one so that you'd be Named."

"Please!" Twig yelled. "Char isn't well! Leave him alone!"

Burdock would have none of it. "Get back!" he barked. "I've got him. Basil, get over to that side. We'll come from two directions. Take this end of the rope!"

But suddenly Burdock saw Twig's masterpiece on one side of the room.

The delicately soldered workings, the balanced arms, the weights, the glistening hinges, and shiny orbs were all wired with copper, brass, silver, and iron. The seemingly nonsensical uselessness of it irritated Burdock. His eyes darted around the room until he saw what he needed. A hammer.

"So you've had help with your projects?" he barked. "This is what I think of your projects!"

"No!" Twig cried out.

Burdock grabbed the hammer and began striking at Twig's project. Pieces of metal flew through the air. Gears and levers were mangled and bent.

Char snapped to attention with a snort. Using what

little strength he had, he
flapped toward Bur-
dock, with wings
vibrating and

stretched out—lifting off the ground and flying for the
first time. His eyes were once again flames of orange
and yellow, his scales undulating, his tail flicking and
twisting. The dragon opened its bright-pink mouth in a
hiss. He let out a strange, growling, gurgling sound that
surprised even Twig.

And then it happened.

The scales on Char's neck stuck out, perpendicular to his body. His mouth opened wider, and he lowered his head close to the floor. He snorted again, and out came a flame that made his past fire breathing seem like a damp match. The entire room lit up with blue-white light as fire rushed out of the dragon with a roar.

Lily shrieked, and Burdock yelped, backing away and dropping the hammer.

Then Char reared back again and sent another flame directly at Burdock, hitting him in the shoulder.

"AAH!" he screamed, wincing in pain, clutching at the burned patch. The smell of scorched fur filled the room.

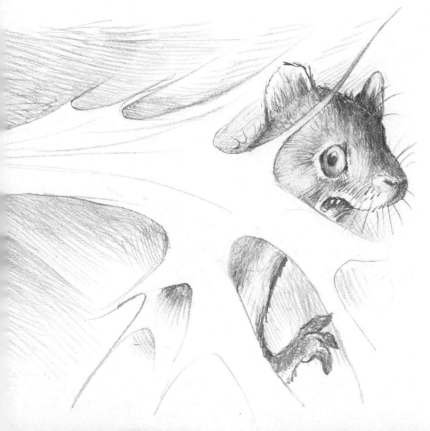

Wings vibrating, Char came at Burdock again. The weasel backed away until he was cornered against the wall.

"Help!" Burdock screeched.

Char snorted fire again, but suddenly the flames had faded a bit and were a pale yellow. Twig could sense that the dragon was rapidly losing strength.

"Char! Stop!" Twig yelled.

The dragon turned and looked at Twig, then back at Burdock, defeated. Thick smoke curled out of his nostrils, gray-green, blue, and brown. Char was breathing in harsh bursts. His eyes seemed slightly sunken, his scales ashy and dull.

He had used up his last bit of energy and was now defenseless. He lay on the floor. Twig and Lily ran to the dragon; Lily cradled the creature's head and neck in her lap.

Olive was rounding a bend in the path when she heard the loud burst of flame, and then Burdock's scream. She raced into the clock tower to see Burdock panting and seething. He glared at Olive.

"Look what your son has been hiding from us!" he barked.

Olive saw Twig and Lily crouched around a . . . she wasn't sure what it was, but she knew immediately which side she was on.

"A dragon?" she asked.

"You mean you knew about this?" Burdock asked incredulously.

Olive looked around the room. Although the chaos of the scene suggested the dragon was a menace, she sensed otherwise. She studied her son. Her eyes met his, and she felt in them the devotion Twig had for the dragon. She made a decision.

"Why, yes," Olive answered. "Of course I knew."

Burdock's eyebrows arched up.

"You're telling me that you and Twig had a dragon in your house?"

"Twig is quite devoted to him."

"Devoted? He's a menace to our community. He

must be contained immediately." He rubbed his singed shoulder. "He is dangerous!"

Olive glanced at Burdock's raw patch of fur and could smell the burned hair. "The dragon did that?" she asked quietly, looking quickly at Twig. "He is really quite gentle, if you are gentle with him, that is."

"Of *course* it was the dragon!"

A small group of residents had gathered outside, Beau among them. He hobbled up to the crowd, surveying the scene, and then saw Char, still collapsed in the corner. His watery eyes widened at the sight of the dragon, and he cast a look at Twig.

Burdock growled, glaring at Beau. "That beast nearly killed me. Look at this!" He thrust his shoulder at Twig. Where the fur had singed off, you could see the red and swollen burned skin, raw and oozing pus and blood. "A few inches' difference and this could have been my face!"

"I—I—I'm sorry, Master Burdock," Twig stammered. "Char is so protective of me, of the project . . . I guess he went a little crazy."

"He needs to be locked up. And his fire-breathing abilities can be utilized, for the good of the Hill."

"What do you mean?" asked Twig. "What are you going to do with him?"

"The dragon's fire can be harnessed. . . . We can use it. Imagine what I—I mean, what the Hill—can create with this beast. He's something the Hill can use."

Twig's heart raced, and he gulped with guilt. He thought of how he had used Char for his projects, and how Char had trusted in him and eagerly helped. Now it was his turn to come to Char's rescue.

"We can take this whole matter before the Council

if you like, Professor Burdock," Beau said calmly. "But let's not lose our tempers and—"

"Fine for you to say!" Burdock interjected. "You weren't nearly roasted by this walking blowtorch. I'm using my authority as a Judiciary Committee member to imprison this beast before one more Hill member is harmed."

Beau raised his paws. "He looks to me to be quite a creature." He nodded at Twig. "And the boy certainly has at least some control over him. Do you really think he needs to be confined?"

"I can take full responsibility for him," Olive suggested.

Twig looked gratefully at both his mother and Beau. Beau gave him a reassuring wink.

"I'm taking him away!" Burdock growled. He grabbed the rope and thrust it at Twig. "Tie this around him!" He winced and clutched his wounded shoulder. "I wouldn't be surprised if a special meeting was called to decide if you should be expelled . . . permanently. I know that I am personally going to recommend just that."

Twig glanced at Lily, who looked on the verge of tears, as Basil looped the rope around Char's neck.

"And let's not forget," he snickered, his dark eyes staring into Twig, "how you lied and cheated to have this beast do all your work. No wonder your assignments were so much better than your classroom ones! You had help! Well, the Council and the rest of the Hill won't stand for it. I wouldn't be surprised if you are expelled on the spot. I'd start packing a bag if I were you. Come, Basil, help me get this creature locked up."

Basil cautiously gave the rope a short tug. Char looked at Twig, perplexed, and didn't budge.

Twig gave him a gentle pat. "It's okay, Char. I'll come to see you later."

Burdock snorted. "The only time *you'll* ever see him is when you visit the Burrow of Confinement. Olive . . . Lily . . . be ready for an inquest into your part in this," the weasel added with a cold smile.

The dragon stood up, painfully, as Basil yanked him out the doorway.

Lily's father had arrived, and he grabbed her by the paw and pulled her away. The rest of the gathered throng parted, gazing and gasping at the sight, as Burdock and Basil led Char toward the Burrow of Confinement.

chapter 19

A Plan

Olive studied her son. "Twig," she said. "Maybe you'd better start at the beginning. Where did Char come from? Where did you find him? Why didn't you tell us about him?"

Beau nodded gravely. "Yes, Twig. I think you need to tell us everything. From the beginning."

Twig sat on the floor, relieved. It felt good to finally tell about all the events of the past few weeks . . . of nearly drowning in the giant river, of discovering the beautiful golden sphere that turned out to be Char's egg, and of keeping Char a secret.

"But why keep him hidden away?" Olive asked. "You can see how that turned out to be a bad idea. I might have been able to help you."

"I was afraid they'd take him away," Twig answered quietly. "And . . . he was my friend."

"Twig, you were wrong to use Char as a way to get ahead in class," Olive replied. "I agree, having him in the Burrow of Confinement doesn't seem fair, but right now we have to think about you. There could be serious consequences . . . for you, me, Lily . . . but definitely you."

"I'm going to go before the rest of the Council and ask for leniency," Beau said. "But Burdock has vengeance on his mind. I can only try my best to persuade them to let you stay." He looked straight at Twig. "It's doubtful that you'll ever be part of the Naming Ceremony."

Twig nodded. He did realize that his chances of becoming Twig Metal Crafter were now next to zero. At best, he would be a Permanent Apprentice, or possibly Assistant. More likely was Errand Runner.

"It's so unfair," he said, all at once exasperated and frustrated and exhausted. "So what if I can't be a Master Metal Crafter? Maybe I just wasn't cut out to be that. Maybe I am cut out for something else. I just don't know what . . . not yet."

Beau picked up some of the debris on the floor. "Could you be an Errand Runner and be happy?" he asked.

"I don't know. I feel like one already," Twig replied. "I think I've felt that way for as long as I can remember . . . always worrying about what everyone on the Hill thinks of me, how they think I'm a failure, or don't fit in. And always, always comparing me to my father. Doesn't anyone like me for being just . . . *me*?"

Olive smiled. She smoothed out Twig's furry topknot, gently brushed some bits of ash out of his whiskers. "You're so much like your father in so many ways," she said.

"Like what?"

"Your perseverance," she replied. "Your devotion. Your gentle spirit. Those are all great, great qualities. So much more important than craftsmanship. At the end of the day, what really matters is the love others have for you. Great skill at something is a wonderful thing, don't get me wrong, but there is no comparing it to being a great friend. I think you're being just that. Your devotion and kindness to Char, and being a good friend to Lily . . . those are things that determine greatness. Those are things that come from you just being . . . *you*."

Twig looked at his mother. "I guess I should be worried about my possible expulsion, about never being Master anything, but right now all I can think about is poor Char!"

Olive studied her son. There was maturity in his eyes she hadn't noticed before. "The Committee is a powerful group," she said. "But somehow I think you'll be fine. Find your heart. You'll do the right thing."

Twig smiled, then thought for a moment. "I've got to go to Lily's," he said. "I won't be long." And with a swoosh of his tail, he was gone.

LILY WAS AT HER DEN, SITTING WITH HER PARENTS, WHEN Twig rapped on her door.

"Excuse me," he said, embarrassed. "I'm sorry . . . but Lily, can I see you for a minute?"

Lily's father looked at Twig a little sadly. "Twig," he said. "Lily has been telling us about what happened, this incredible story about a dragon, practically killing Master Burdock, setting fire to . . . well, I'm sure it was all an accident, but to tell you the truth, we'd rather not have Lily involved in this. She's guilty by association, you might say. I'd prefer if Lily didn't see you, at least until this whole thing blows over."

"What?" Twig exclaimed. He looked at Lily, who sat, miserable, at the table, as though she had just been fed skunk cabbage.

Lily returned his glance and then spoke. "Dad,

202

Mom, could I just talk to Twig for one minute? I promise I'll be right back."

Her father nodded sternly. "Just for a minute," he relented. "I'm sure Twig will be wanting to get back home. Am I right, Twig?" He looked at Twig suggestively.

Twig nodded. Then he and Lily slipped outside.

"I can't believe this," Twig said.

"Poor Char," Lily whispered. "The thought of him in the Burrow of Confinement . . . we've got to get him out."

Twig stared at Lily. "Get him out? Like, break him out?"

"If we don't, who will? And if no one does, what will happen to him?" she replied emphatically.

"You're right, Lily. It wasn't right for me to keep

him here. It's up to us. We've got to get Char back home. He'll be like a slave if he stays here."

"Back home? Back home where? Where's home?"

"Well, I don't know, exactly. But it must be somewhere near where I found his egg. I can get us that far at least." He looked questioningly at her. "Lily, would you come? All the way to the big river?"

Lily's eyes flashed with anticipation. "Of course I will! Look, I'm in this, too. And Char . . . Char is like family now. We can't let him down."

"What will you tell your parents?"

"They'll be okay . . . the important thing now is Char."

Twig nodded. "Meet me at the prison as soon as you can," he whispered. "And bring some supplies . . . you know, food . . . whatever you can bring."

Just then Lily's father poked his whiskers out the burrow door. "What are you two up to?" he asked. "Lily, time to come inside."

"Just one more second, Dad," Lily answered.

"No, now," her father said.

"Okay." Lily glanced knowingly at Twig and flicked her tail.

chapter 20

Escape

The Burrow of Confinement sat at the edge of the Hill, in an area seldom used. Tall weeds surrounded an old metal box.

Twig and Lily looked around cautiously.

"Coast is clear," Twig said. "Now the hard part. . . . How do we break Char out?"

He tapped lightly on the giant metal door and heard the muffled stirring of Char inside.

"Char?" Lily whispered. "It's okay . . . we've come to rescue you." She looked doubtfully at the huge padlock.

"Twig, I don't know how we can break through this. If we had Char and his flamethrower, we could work on the lock, but he's on the wrong side of the problem."

Just then a voice spoke behind them.

"You need this?"

Twig and Lily pivoted on their toes. There stood Basil, smiling nonchalantly, dangling a large silver key on a long chain.

"Basil!" they said in unison.

"Who else?" replied Basil. "Obviously you two need some help, somebody with the right connections."

Twig clenched his paws and frowned. "Basil, you can't stop us from helping Char escape. He's done nothing wrong, really, and—"

Basil swung the key in the air. "Do you see this?" he asked. "This, my friends, is the one key—the only

key—to the lock that holds Char behind bars."

Lily blinked, and then her eyes widened. "Basil, you're actually helping? You want Char to escape?"

"Maybe," Basil replied.

Twig knew they had to act quickly to free Char. It

was possible that the Council members would be there any minute.

"How did you get the key?" Twig asked.

Basil smiled. "My uncle had the key, as head of the Guild Judiciary Committee. I just found the right moment to slip it out of his desk drawer . . . easy as pie."

"May I have it, Basil?" Twig asked directly. "Will you give it to me, please?"

"Why should I?" replied Basil.

Twig knew that Basil was just playing with them. The padlock was high-grade steel and looked formidable. Twig and Lily looked at each other.

"Char is sick," Twig said. "We've got to get him back to where he's from. Soon. Before the Committee takes him. We need the key. Will you help us, Basil?"

Basil hesitated, then tossed the key to Twig. Twig shot him a look of gratitude.

The silver key opened the padlock with a *click*, and they heaved open the heavy door. Char scrambled out, his wings flapping weakly.

Twig hugged him gently. "Hey, buddy!" he murmured.

Char's tongue darted out, tickling Twig's ear. Then he began sniffing Basil's whiskers.

"Hey! Stop it!" Basil said. He started giggling as Char's snout covered his face.

"See? He likes you," said Lily. "He knows a friend when he sees one."

"He's a maniac!" Basil squeaked, obviously enjoying Char's attention.

Twig glanced around anxiously. "We'd better get moving," he said. "Are you coming, Basil?"

The weasel smiled. "Of course I'm coming, Woodpecker Toes."

Twig grinned back. "We need to make one quick stop before we head out. This way."

They raced to his house and found it empty. Twig scampered into his room, grabbed his beloved *Dragons* book, and turned to his favorite page. He left the book open, where he knew Olive would see it, and quickly penciled a note. *Home soon. Love, Twig.*

Hurrying back outside, he gestured to his friends. Then they quickly slipped beneath a grove of may-apples and were gone.

chapter 21

The River

Twig turned, looking in all directions, orienting himself.

"This looks right," he said. "I know this is the way. See that poplar tree? The one with the split trunk? I remember that tree."

"What's that prove?" Basil questioned.

"The poplar wasn't far from the river. There was a large rock on the other side of it. We head this way, the sun to our backs. I'm betting that we'll be at the river before dark."

They scrambled beneath the spicebush and wild ginger to the base of the ancient poplar. The three friends arched their heads back, looking up, up, up to the very distant branches, high above the forest floor. The tree, strikingly massive, was an excellent landmark, with a smooth, gray trunk that stretched a hundred feet above them. Twig hurriedly skirted the roots of the tree to the other side.

"Yes! It's here!" he called out. "The rock, the large patch of ferns . . . it's all here, just like I remember!"

Lily hopped over one of the massive roots and joined him. "Good job, Twig," she said.

From their vantage point, out from beneath the brambles and wild ginger and mayapples, he could sense they were getting close. With the green-yellow dappled sunlight warming his whiskers, Twig felt exhilarated. He lifted his nose into the sweet-smelling breeze. Something foreign, yet familiar, tickled his whiskers and pulled at his heart.

"This way!" He pointed. "Can you smell it in the air? That's the river. We're not far now!"

They set off, the sun behind them, heading east. The tall trees, mostly poplar and beech, stretched above them like canyon walls, their highest branches in another world of sunrises, sunsets, lightning storms, drifting clouds, and soaring hawks.

The air grew saltier, carried on a breeze in little puffs that glided across the marsh grasses. Suddenly, just as Twig remembered from before, the trees opened up to a vast, late-afternoon sky, and the three friends

found themselves high up on a cliff. The unobstructed
breeze rushed at them, rippling their fur, blowing their
whiskers back, and they looked at one another, amazed,
laughing and pointing. The sky was an intense cobalt
blue, with puffs of white that slid across the blue like
skaters on ice. Circling gulls called out, banking and
gliding on the fresh wind.

"I've never . . . wow!" stuttered Lily. "You can see . . . everywhere!"

Even Basil couldn't control his excitement. "It's amazing!" he exclaimed. "Look, there! You can see the river bending. Where does it go? And look . . . as far as the eye takes you . . . so much sky!"

The three sat on the embankment, nibbling on sweet green grass, staring at the scene stretching out in front of them. Char lay in the weeds, his nose pointing into the breeze. Lily scanned the river far below them.

"Is this where you found Char?" she asked.

"Near here," replied Twig. "By the way, be careful. The edge of the embankment can collapse in a second. I don't want to fall into the river again."

Basil and Lily exchanged a nervous glance, and then backed slightly away from the cliff.

"Well, what do we do now?" Basil asked.

"We figure out a way to get Char back home, wherever that is," Twig answered. The three of them studied the river as it flowed at the bottom of the steep cliff. They noticed the huge piles of flotsam that had accumulated and piled against the riverbank. Tons of driftwood and debris had been deposited over the years and years of high tides, creating dunes and hills and floes . . . a scavenger's delight.

Char lifted his nose into the air as though smelling something familiar, but his wings hung limp and frail and his coloring had become worse, even more ashy and dull. The seriousness of their adventure suddenly hit them hard.

"Well," Twig said finally. "We aren't helping Char

get better by sitting here." He nodded at the river and the piles of debris. "This is a tidal river. It ebbs and flows. That's how we're getting Char home. All that stuff floated in and was left here. I bet Char's egg floated in the same way. We need to follow the tide back out."

"I don't know anything about rivers," Lily said.

"Hey, me neither," added Basil. "This looks dangerous. What makes you think we can just float out to sea, like it was nothing?"

"I didn't say that," Twig answered. "I just know we have to. We may have to build a boat."

"Build a boat," Basil grumbled. "Just like that. Build a boat and float down the river."

Lily giggled.

"Yes," Twig replied calmly.

"We don't know anything about building a boat," Basil snorted.

"What about supplies?" Lily asked. "Materials? And food? We'll have to take food with us, so we'll have to store some up. There's no telling how far we're going.

Or for how long," she added wistfully. "But I can see boards . . . and pieces of rope . . . and vines. We'll have stuff to use. I bet we can find all sorts of materials in those piles of debris."

Basil's tail twitched. "Won't that take quite a while?" he pondered. "Seems like that'd take forever!"

"Then we'd better get going," Twig replied. "Come on, Char." He patted the dragon gently.

chapter 22

A Discovery

C har was weak and frail, but he lifted his nose into the salty breeze and stretched his wings. It seemed to stir something in him, and he looked a bit more alert and eager. The fresh air was doing him good.

Lily stared down the embankment. "Now the tough part," she said. "Getting down the cliff."

"Yeah, believe me, you don't want to do it like I did it last time," Twig said grimly. "Let's space ourselves out, so we don't put too much weight in one place, or else the dirt may cave in. Hang on to sturdy weeds and roots."

Off the group started, single file, carefully creating a switchback trail as they went. Overhanging vines and branches created handrails, and jutting rocks and roots helped with footing.

They crisscrossed their way downward, the air growing cooler and darker in the shadow of the river-bank. A forest of ironweed, goldenrod, and joe-pye weed towered over them, their flower heads waving in the wind, riotous with magenta and yellow and pink, thick with bees and beetles, butterflies and bugs.

At last the ground leveled out and they began to see, up close, the sea of flotsam around them. It was a landscape of every floatable object imaginable: uncountable plastic cups and plates, wooden boards covered with barnacles, bottles and cans, fishing nets, foam ice chests. . . . It was all here, washed up with the tide and waiting for thousands of years to biodegrade.

Twig, Lily, and Basil stared at the sea of debris around them.

"Imagine what could be made with all these parts," Lily pondered.

"We should have no problem making a boat out of this stuff," Twig agreed. "There must be a million boards and other pieces to use."

"This is craziness," Basil said. "What do we use to put the boards together? To actually build the boat?"

"Well, rope, or cord, to start with," Twig answered. "There's so much stuff . . . we'll be able to figure something out, I'm sure of it."

"Me too, Twig," said Lily. "If we spread out, looking for good supplies, we can cover more territory. Let's bring anything useful back here. If it's too big for one, then give a yell and we'll all come to help."

Off they went, in different directions, Char lying in the shade of some mallow. Soon, from inside a thicket of reeds, Basil gave a yell.

"Over here!" he cried.

Twig and Lily raced over to find Basil perched on a large, irregularly shaped piece of packing foam, lodged in the weeds.

"See?" he said happily. "It's light, we can carry it,

and it will float beautifully. Perfect!"

Lily looked dubious. "You really think? Will it hold all of us?"

"One way to find out," Twig said. "Let's get it to the water and test it out."

The three friends lifted the Styrofoam piece easily and started toward the water's edge.

"Almost there!" urged Twig. He felt himself slip a little. "Hey! My feet are sliding! It's muddy! We must be close!"

Snagging on weeds and drift-wood pieces, they pulled the Styro-foam craft to the riverbank. It floated, but it proved too unsteady to be used as a boat; it rolled and pitched at the slightest movement, throwing all three of its crew into the water. Disappointed, they sat on the bank, studying the problematic boat.

"What if we added a float on each side, to steady it?" suggested Twig.

Lily thought for a second. "That might work," she said.

"I saw some other pieces of the foam, out in the piles of stuff," Basil added. "I bet if we find some other pieces and attach them to sticks, we could make side boats that would keep everything steady. Steady enough to take us downriver, anyway."

The three of them set off into the mountain of debris, eyes peeled for possible pontoons. And then they saw it.

A huge glass bottle sat in front of them, partially tilted to one side, half in mud, half in the water, a giant cork in the neck end. Barnacles and algae grew along the bottom of the bottle, crusted and thick from ages spent floating in the water. The glass was dirty after sitting in the silt and mud, but the treasure inside was clear enough.

The tall, dark shape of a beautiful sailboat loomed above them.

"Do you see what I see?" Lily gasped.

"It's . . . a ship!" murmured Twig. "Like a picture in a book, but much better . . . because it's real!"

Lily spit on her paw and wiped away a bit of the mud. "I can see little round windows. And ropes going down the side. It's even got a flag!"

Twig and Basil hurried to Lily's side and wiped their own windows in the glass.

"And it looks like it's in good shape," Twig added.

Lily raced around to another spot. "Over here!" she called out. "I can see a name on it."

"*Captive*," Twig whispered. "It's beautiful!"

"It looks like one of the sails collapsed," observed Basil.

"That can be fixed, I'm sure," said Twig. "It'll work!"

Basil jerked his head around. "Work how?"

"It'll work for our boat, of course," Twig replied. "To get Char home."

"You mean float down the river in this?" Basil gasped.

"Sure! Why not?" Twig said. "It's the perfect thing! A boat already made for us! I saw one just like it in a book."

"Yeah, well, maybe, except for one thing," Basil said. "It's trapped in a bottle."

He tapped the glass. "This stuff is thick. We couldn't break it open if we tried."

Twig let out a sigh of disappointment. The three sat in silence, pondering the situation, gazing at the towering boat.

Suddenly Lily let out a little chirp. "Hey! What about Char?"

"What?" Twig asked.

"Char! Char can blast through this glass. This is nothing to him. We'll use him to free the boat."

"That's it!" Twig chittered.

"We don't know if it even floats," Basil said.

"We'll test it," Twig replied. He looked at Char a little doubtfully, gently stroking the dragon's neck. "Char, buddy? Are you well enough? Can you handle this job?" He looked at the others. "We can try using Char to free the boat, but if he gets much worse, we'll have to find another way. We can't risk his life. Agreed?"

"Agreed," Lily and Basil said in unison.

Twig grinned. "Let's free the *Captive*!"

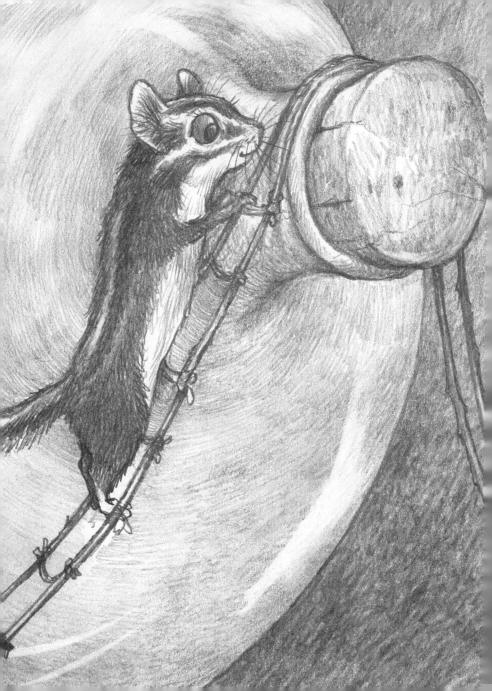

chapter 23

Getting Things Shipshape

They got to work.

"Idea," Twig said. "What if we cut through the cork of the bottle first? That will let us go in, check out the *Captive*, and see what needs to be done."

"Sounds good," Basil agreed.

Lily found honeysuckle and creeper vines and deftly wove them into a rope ladder, looped on one end. She tossed the looped end over the bottle's neck, and in several tries, the ladder was finally in place. Twig climbed up and tapped on the cork.

"This will be a cinch for Char," he called down. "Lily, show Char where to aim."

Lily coaxed Char, who made a clicking sound in his throat, and then coughed, but there was only a bit of yellow flame. He gasped and panted. It was enough to weaken the cork, but only that.

Twig examined the remaining cork. "I think I can handle the rest of this!" he shouted down. "But Char can't take on the glass bottle. We'll have to have another plan for that."

Twig chewed and clawed at the rest of the cork stopper. The crumbly bits of cork fell away, and soon he could poke his head inside. The air was musty, but dry. He slid down into the inside of the bottle, landing with a thump against the bow of the boat. The proud ship arched above him. He felt a tingle up his tail.

He turned and tapped the glass. "It's okay!" he hollered. "Come on in!" Basil and Lily could hear his muffled voice behind the thick glass. They scrambled up the ladder, then slid down the glass as Twig had done.

"A little beat up, but I think maybe we can work with this," said Basil, looking up. "Some of the ropes are dry-rotted, but the sails look good."

"And this part seems sound as a nut," said Twig, tapping on the hull.

The boat was perched on a wooden platform, which had its brass nameplate tacked to it, barely legible under a mask of tarnish. Some of the rigging had come loose, cascading down the side of the bow, and they climbed up.

"It's magnificent!" Lily sighed as they explored the deck. "Look at the craftsmanship. The carving. And the brass! Imagine how this ship would look after a good overhauling."

Basil found the wheel and gave it a turn. A loud squeak came from behind and below, and Twig and Lily scurried to the stern.

"Do that again!" Twig yelled out. Looking down, he and Lily could see the brass rudder, stiff from inactivity, squeaky and grumbly, but still very much in working order.

"I bet that's how you steer it," Lily said. "A little work and we'll have the *Captive* good as new. First, the rope work. I'll handle that." She made a mental list of what needed repair or replacing and then got to work refitting the rigging.

With her mastery of knots and ropes, the work went quickly. She used old fishing nets and nylon line to create a rope bridge from the ground to the bow, new rope ladders to the tiny crow's nest, and new lashings and bindings so the sails were tight and strong.

Twig and Basil gave the hull a good going-over, looking for any cracks or holes that could cause leaks when the *Captive* was afloat.

Basil found an old tube of toothpaste, mostly squeezed out. With a bit of rag he used it to polish the old brass to a new gleam.

They found a vegetable oil bottle floating in the debris and used the remaining dab of oil inside to lubricate the rudder. They polished and wiped and swabbed and dusted until the *Captive* was as majestic as the day she was built. With everyone working, it wasn't long before the ship was refitted, stem to stern.

"How do you figure we'll get her in the water?" Basil asked.

Twig nodded solemnly. "I know. . . . The *Captive*

is a big boat. But I'll think of something."

"*We'll* think of something," Basil replied. "Three heads are better than one."

Twig grinned. *This is better than any Naming Ceremony,* he thought. *Building friends is better than building things.*

Char, who had spent the time mostly napping in the shade, still looked gray and frail, but the fresh breeze was working a bit of magic on him; his health had not greatly improved, but it had not declined, either. His eyes seemed a bit clearer, and he looked repeatedly toward the east. Twig felt that, somehow, Char knew he was nearer home, and that was keeping his decline at bay. And that made Twig work all the harder at preparing the *Captive* for its maiden voyage.

Now it was just a matter of getting the *Captive* into the water.

chapter 24

Freedom

They contemplated how they could break the glass bottle. Twig wandered through the piles of debris, lost in thought. He scrambled over what he thought was a pile of sticks and driftwood, but something else caught his eye. The handle of a hammer, long ago separated from its claw, poked out from the mass of wood pieces. Twig's mind raced: What if they *made* a hammer, then used it to smash the glass?

"Hey! Over here!" he squealed as he pulled at the wooden handle.

Basil took one look, and his whiskers lit up. "Got it!" he exclaimed.

"Got it!" Lily joined in. "We find something to use as a weight, fasten it to the handle, and create a glass smasher. Right?"

"Right," Twig replied. "Lily, you find all the rope and vines we'll need. Basil and I will search for the right weight. Let's go!"

Lily scrambled over logs and rocks and debris, searching for the long lengths of twine and fishing line and honeysuckle vines that she'd need. Basil and Twig unearthed a long, oddly shaped rock that seemed perfect. It took them a while, but pushing in unison, they got it into position. Then, tying one end of the rope to

the rock, they made a swinging hammer. After many attempts, they had the hammer suspended, dangling from an overhanging tree limb.

The other end of the rope was tied down. The three of them pulled the rock up a slope, then let go. The rock swung in a deep arc, swooshing through the weeds and hitting the glass bottle with a hard *whack!*

After several blows the thick glass cracked, then cracked some more, then shattered in hundreds of shards. Twig and Basil tied the larger pieces with ropes and dragged them away from the area. Lily gingerly cleared the deck of broken pieces, tossing them over the side, and then swept the planks of the deck clean.

The ship was finally free from the bottle. For the

first time, a breeze rippled and caressed the sails softly. The setting sun glinted off the shiny brass fittings and polished deck before sinking below the trees.

"It's magnificent," Lily said, reverently looking up at the ship.

"Agreed," Twig replied.

"We did it!" Basil added.

They stood watching as a magnificent, golden-orange full moon tiptoed above the treetops; Twig couldn't remember it ever being so huge, feeling so near. He scampered to the rope ladder, and almost immediately splashed into ankle-deep water.

"Wha . . . ?" he gasped. "Water here?" Only a short time before, it had been a muddy path.

He thought quickly. "Okay, everyone, we need to move fast. You two grab all the food and supplies you can. Make as many trips as you need to. Find some sticks and rags. . . . We'll make torches so we can see better. I'm getting Char. We have to get on the boat!"

Lily looked wide-eyed. "Now?"

"Yes. The river is rising. Look—you can see stuff floating in. We have to move fast!"

IN A MATTER OF MINUTES THE THREE WERE GATHERING food and all the extra supplies they could handle and were transferring them, like a bucket brigade, onto the deck of the *Captive*.

"Elderberries," Lily said, handing up a woven grass basket of the dark-purple fruit. Then she tossed acorn after acorn to Basil, like it was a game of catch, until the hold of the ship was nearly full.

Char climbed nimbly up the rope ladder, with Twig's help, flapping his wings to keep balance. Meanwhile the water rose higher still, coming up to Lily's chest, as she struggled to keep the supplies over her head, high and dry.

"Why are we doing this? In the middle of the night? Why don't we wait for the water to drop again?" Basil asked, lifting a canteen of fresh water onto the deck.

Twig glanced at him seriously. "If my guess is correct, you'll see why in about half an hour," he replied.

The moon was relentlessly pulling at the river water, which lapped at the base of the *Captive*. The wooden stand with the brass nameplate was now a dozen centimeters under water, and still the water rose. Suddenly, the ship shifted with a jerk, sending Twig and Basil sprawling on the deck. Lily grabbed the railing and looked down.

"Uh-oh!" she shouted.

"What happened? What was that?" Basil called out.

"The water is moving against the ship. . . . It's lifting the ship up."

Another jerk, this time harder than the first, sent the boat sliding and scraping along the muddy bottom and lifted it free from the wooden base.

The three friends gathered at the bow, staring off into the darkness. Tall weeds, a jungle of obstacles, surrounded them. "This is it!" Twig yelled out. "Everybody, man your station! Char, hang on! Lily, Basil, hold the torch out in front, left and right. I'll take the wheel. Call out directions so we don't hit anything."

"Floating log, straight ahead!" shouted Basil. He pointed to the left. "Turn that way! Nasty-looking tree branch up ahead!"

All through the early-morning hours they dodged and meandered their way through the forest of weeds, driftwood, and rocks. Somehow, even as the treacherous branches and debris threatened them, Twig realized that this was his dream: gripping the wheel of the *Captive* and steering his way, returning Char to his home. He thought of how proud his father would be of him now, confidently guiding a ship through obstacles into open water.

Twig thought to himself: *Sometimes the things we want and the things we love get tangled up in our hearts like bramble when we try to do what's right.*

He glanced at the dragon. The river air was working like a tonic. Char still looked frail, but it was

encouraging to see him lift his head from the deck and sniff into the breeze and flutter his wings a bit.

Lily seemed to read his thoughts. "Char's looking better already," she called out, smiling. Twig grinned back and nodded.

The tide, now slowly returning the river to the sea, was pulling them out, into a stronger current. The sky opened up above them. A pale mauve dawn emerged in the east as the *Captive* made its way through the last of the river's-edge obstacles. The dangerous rocks and piles of flotsam were behind them now. An early-morning breeze fluttered its way onto the canvas sails. Twig turned the wheel, and the ship pointed toward the dawn.

There was a mist hanging low on the river, and tiny dew droplets clung to Twig's fur. Lily moved beside him, handing him a small wild cherry, and he happily munched at the sweet fruit.

The breeze picked up. The sails billowed out, and the *Captive* danced lightly over the green-gray water.

The first birdcall of the day, a woodpecker far off in the shrouded woods, echoed across the water. The mist was dissipating. Twig looked at Lily, and she smiled.

The river was calling them.

◆ TWIG'S ADVENTURE CONTINUES IN THE SEQUEL TO ◆

Brambleheart

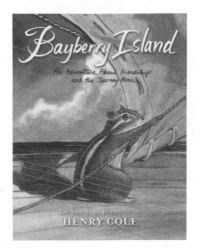

chapter 1

The *Spirit*

Twig's furry paws were sore. Gripping the spokes of the *Spirit*'s wheel for three days had turned his pads from pink and tender to tough and calloused.

His body was sore, too. The *Spirit* had sailed through a maze of floating debris and an endless series of rapids, with Twig guiding her every mile. His arms twitched from exhaustion.

His legs were tired from balancing. Tiny scratches marked where his toes had gripped the wooden planks of the deck.

But Twig's confidence had grown, as well as his muscles.

He gazed ahead, alert, looking for floating hazards and telltale signs of ripples and rapids. Things that had seemed so foreign just a few days ago were now a part of him: the patterns of water currents, the shadows of the clouds, even the smell of the river was like a friend.

A shout came from the crow's nest above him. "Looks like a log up ahead, on the right!" Basil was at his usual perch, with legs and tail dangling through the rails.

"Yep, I see it!" Twig shouted back. "Thanks, Basil!"

"When do we get to wherever we're going?" the weasel called down. "Can't we pull ashore somewhere?"

Lily stepped beside Twig, grinning. "How about it, Twig?" she said. "Want me to relieve you at the wheel? Then you can take the crow's nest and Basil can rest. He's still looking a little woozy."

Twig and Lily were quite adept at life on the water, but Basil had had a tougher time finding his sea legs. The swaying of the mast as the wind rippled the sails didn't help.

Lily glanced toward the rear of the ship. "And Char could use some attention," she added.

Char lay draped and drooping across the deck of the ship, eyes half-lidded, and his scaly skin grayish and dull.

Twig looked at the dragon. "I thought the fresh

air was doing him good, but now I'm not so sure. He looked better three days ago."

"I know," Lily replied. "I keep hoping we'll see some signs that we're close . . . close to finding Char's home."

Twig nodded, then shouted up to the crow's nest. "Come on down, Basil. We're switching off!"

Basil made his shaky way down the rope ladder from the crow's nest. He looked green.

"Can't you make the *Spirit* stand still?" he moaned. "I feel like I've been swinging on a vine for three days."

Lily handed Basil a rose hip. "Here. Chew on this. It may help settle your stomach."

Basil, looking queasy, munched halfheartedly on the rose hip, and Twig sat beside Char. He stroked the dragon's smooth scales and scratched under his chin. Char seemed to barely notice. "Lily, he's not doing so great. I hope we're going in the right direction . . . for Char's sake!"

Lily nodded solemnly. "Let's get him home." She

took her position at the ship's wheel.

Twig thought, for the hundredth time, of home. He missed the delicious meals prepared by his mother, Olive, and the cozy comfort of his cottony bed.

He missed his conversations with Beau and wondered what Beau would think of him now. Would he approve of sailing off to an unknown destination, just to deliver a baby dragon to his home? "Beau would be proud of me . . . I know he would," Twig said to himself.

Even though their days had been busy, Twig knew that in between learning to sail and exploring the river, Lily was missing home, too. A pang of guilt passed through his thoughts. If it weren't for him, and his discovery of Char, they'd both be safe at home, not on the *Spirit*, in the middle of the river.

He scampered up to the crow's nest and tipped his nose into the breeze. The scent of the river made his spine tingle with pleasure. Water gushing over stones and swirling between rocks was like music to him. Dozens of bright-blue damselflies came to rest on the railing of the *Spirit*, and jittery water striders skittered out of the way as the ship plowed past.

The view from atop the mast was exhilarating. The river had widened, opening up their view. He'd never seen such an expanse of sky before, with only a few distant trees obstructing the panorama. The evening before they had sat on the deck of the ship and watched, enraptured: the setting sun turned a scattering of clouds into a gold-and-orange necklace above the dark-purple horizon.

And the vegetation was different than it had been upriver. The tangle of vines along the cliffs and banks had given way to prickly shrubs and tall, rippling grasses.

Twig scanned the horizon ahead. "Keep her steady!" he shouted to Lily below.

"You got it!" Lily called back. "Twig, am I imagining things, or does the current seem slower? We seem to be slowing down!"

Twig watched the bow of the ship as it sliced through the water. A breeze was pushing at the sails, but the water was like glass. "You're right, Lily. There is definitely less current."

Far off in the distance he saw a hazy line stretching across the river. As the wind nudged them closer and closer, he began to make out the jagged shapes of sticks and branches jutting out of the water.

"Something . . . straight ahead!" he squeaked. "Not

sure what it is, but"—he glanced left and right—"I don't see a way around it. It's like a wall!"

Basil seemed to stir from his woozy lethargy. He scampered to the bow. "A wall? Are we going to crash?"

"At the rate we're going, we will," Twig shouted back. "Sails down! We have to slow down! Everybody, grab a rope quickly!"

In a rush the three friends pulled at the series of ropes, working together and rolling the sails up to the masts, then lashing them down. As they worked, the *Spirit* slowed some, but still drifted toward the dangerous line of branches.

"Oh my gosh!" Lily squeaked. Her ears cocked forward in alarm. "We're heading right into it!"

"Keep working at the sails, Lily. We're slowing down. . . . I think we may stop in time!"

Little by little, the ship slowed, and the last sail was tied to its mast. Finally the *Spirit* sat still in the water.

The evening breeze had died. Twig raced to the bow of the ship, gripping the railing. "It's a wall!" he

murmured as Lily and Basil joined him. They stared at
the massive tangle of limbs. "A wall of trees!"

chapter 2

Rose Hips and River Water

The sun was just dipping below the horizon; darkness would soon be upon them. There was no reason to try to explore the wall or find any way around it. Basil set the anchor for the night.

Nervous about the barricade looming over them, and chilled by the nighttime air, they tossed uneasily on the deck of the ship, sleeping fitfully when they could. It was still dark when they heard the first distant morning birdsong. They stretched, shivering and stiff.

Lily sent a bucket over the railing and hauled some

water up, as Twig examined their cache of food. "Looks like the last of it," he said. "We're going to have to find some more food soon. We have a few rose hips left, and some acorns. Not much."

"Rose hips and river water, rose hips and river water," Lily said. "Wouldn't a nice, steaming cup of sassafras tea be good right about now?" She smiled wistfully. "And a walnut muffin?"

Basil frowned at her. Being seasick had made him thin, and grouchy. "Please. Don't mention food."

From the deck, Twig and Lily nibbled acorns and examined the giant wall. In the dim morning light they could see that the wall stretched from one side of the river to the other, an enormous distance. It was constructed of thousands of branches and limbs and sticks. Mud was chinked in between, and in many places grasses and weeds and small trees had taken root in the mud. The massive structure towered above them.

Just then the morning sun poured onto the river, illuminating the landscape. "It's a beaver dam!" Lily exclaimed. "Just like Professor Fern told us about. I've never seen one, but that's got to be what it is!"

Twig grinned. "Of course!"

"Well, what good does that do us, knowing that it's a beaver dam?" Basil said. "We're still blocked. We can't go forward and we can't back up. We're stuck."

Twig looked thoughtfully at the dam. "Maybe if we get on top of it, we can see if there's a way around it."

"How are you going to do that, Twig?" Lily asked.

"I'm going to jump. From the crow's nest I can make it to that overhanging branch. See?" He pointed to a sturdy-looking limb that jutted out closest to the *Spirit*.

With that, Twig scurried up the rope ladder to the crow's nest. The jutting branch was tantalizingly close, but dangerously distant.

"Are you sure you can do this?" Basil called up.

"We'll find out!" Twig called back.

"Gruk!" croaked Char with concern.

Just as Twig was crouched and ready to leap, another voice called out.

"Hello!"

They looked up to see the cheerful face of a beaver beaming at them from the top of the dam. "Hello there!" it said again.

"Hello!" shouted Lily. "Good morning!"

The beaver was dark and slick as it moved agilely over the mountain of branches and made its way to the edge of the river. "Good morning to you!" The beaver stared at the *Spirit.* "My, you've found an interesting way of travel! I've never seen such a thing!"

"We're trying to get downriver," Twig explained. "But your dam has blocked our way. Can you help us?"

The beaver looked at the ship. "Hmm. Yep. Think so." With that, it scrambled across the dam, and then returned shortly with a length of grapevine.

"Here! Tie this somewhere, and I'll pull you to a good spot. You'll see!"

Lily lashed the vine to the railing on the bow. "Ready!"

With the other end of the vine in its mouth, the beaver began to tug. Slowly the boat began to move through the water. The beaver ducked under and climbed over and around the myriad of limbs, pulling the *Spirit* along the edge of the dam.

Soon they heard the gushing sound of rushing water. "A break in the dam!" the beaver called out.

"Lucky for you, but on our checklist to repair it today."

"Huh?" Twig shouted.

"Don't worry! You'll make it!"

The current began to carry them through the opening in the dam.

"But careful of the waterfall!" the beaver warned. "The current may be a little strong!"

"Now he tells us!" Basil moaned, grabbing onto the railing.

A torrent of water poured through the break in the beaver dam, and the *Spirit* wobbled and swayed.

"Hold on!" Twig yelled.

Lily gave a yelp. "Whoa!"

The ship pitched and dipped as it was carried

through the dam, down, down, down a series of water-falls and rapids. Several times it nearly capsized, careening side to side.

One sail was snagged on a sharp branch, turning the boat around and causing it to spin in circles.

"Make it stop!" Basil squeaked. "Please make it stop!"

Suddenly, with a splash, the ship plunged through the dam and into the calm water on the other side, the current pushing them along into open water again.

"G'bye! Safe journey!" They turned to see the beaver calling to them from on top of the dam.

"Thank you!" Lily answered back.

The morning sun warmed their backs as they hoisted sails and caught a stiff breeze from the south. Twig's whiskers twitched in the wind. He stood at the wheel and pointed the *Spirit* downriver. It felt good to be moving again.

DON'T MISS THESE BOOKS BY

HENRY COLE

"Evocative illustrations, compelling characters, and thoughtful reflections."
—*Publishers Weekly* (starred review)

"Cole's black-and-white pencil drawings [are] earnest yet emotionally sharp."
—*Kirkus Reviews*

KATHERINE TEGEN BOOKS
An Imprint of HarperCollins *Publishers*

www.harpercollinschildrens.com